LAWFULLY Taken

Elle E. Kay

Faith Writes Publishing

266 Saint Gabriels Rd

Benton, PA 17814

ISBN: 978-0-9994856-3-7

This book is dedicated to my mother who helped develop in me a passion for reading and story.

Introduction to The Lawkeeper Series

There's just something fascinating about a man wearing an emblem of authority. The way the light gleams off that shiny star on his badge makes us stare with respect. Couple that with a uniform hugging his body in just the right way, confidence, and mission to save and protect, it's no wonder we want to know what lies underneath.

Yes, what echoes deep inside those beating hearts is inspiring. Certainly appealing. Definitely enticing. Although those ripped muscles and strong shoulders can make a woman's heart skip a beat—or two—it takes a strong, confident person to choose to love someone who risks it all every day. Anyone willing to become part of a lawkeeper's world might have a story of their own to tell.

The undeniable charisma lawmen possess make all of us pause and take note. It's probably why there are so many movies and TV shows themed around the justice system. We're enthralled by their ability to save babies, help strangers, and rescue damsels in distress. We're captivated by their ability to protect and save, defend the innocent, risk their lives, and face danger without hesitation. Of course, we expect our heroes to stay solid when we're in a mess. We count on them for safety, security, and peace of mind. From yesterday to today, that truth remains constant.

Their valor inspires us, their integrity comforts, and their courage melts our hearts—irresistibly. But there's far more to them than their courageous efforts. How do they deal with the difficulties they face? Can they balance work and life? And how do they find time for love outside their life of service?

We want to invite you on a journey—come with us as we explore the complex lives of the men and women who serve and protect us every day. Join us in a fast-paced world of adventure. Walk into our tight-knit world of close friendships, extended family, and danger—as our super heroes navigate the most treacherous path of all—the road to love.

The Lawkeepers. Historical and modern-day super heroes; men and women of bravery and valor, taking love and law seriously. A multi-author series, sure to lock up your attention and take your heart into custody.

Visit The Lawkeepers on Facebook

Join our mailing list

The Lawkeepers is a multi-author series alternating between

historical westerns and contemporary westerns featuring law enforcement heroes that span multiple agencies and generations. Join bestselling authors Jenna Brandt, Lorana Hoopes, Elle E. Kay, Patricia PacJac Caroll, Evangeline Kelly, Ginny Sterling and Barb Goss as they weave captivating, sweet, and inspirational stories of romance and suspense between the lawkeepers — and the women who love them.

The Lawkeepers is a world like no other; a world where lawkeepers and heroes are honored with unforgettable stories, characters, and love.

** Note: Each book in The Lawkeepers series is a standalone book, and part of a mini-series of sorts, and you can read them in any order.

Chapter 1

January 1883

Adeline stood at the stove heating a pot of venison stew Maria had prepared earlier. She hoped her father's favorite meal would put him in a pleasant mood. Dread filled her at the thought of him spending another night extolling the virtues of marriage and attempting to convince her James Cleveland would be the ideal husband. Mr. Cleveland was a pompous bore. Her parents and caretakers had attempted to imbue in her a sense of duty, but they'd failed. She would not deign to consider a marriage of convenience. She'd prefer to die an old maid.

At the sound of a gunshot, Adeline flew into the adjoining room. The wooden spoon clattered as it hit the floor. Bending over her father, Adeline attempted to stop the bleeding. He'd been shot in the shoulder.

"Get up." The stout bearded man spoke in a low growl.

"No." Adeline made eye contact with the shooter. "I will not."

"Then I'll shoot a hole in that pretty little redhead of yours."

"Go ahead." She tore a piece off her petticoat and tied it around the wound. "I'll not leave my father's side willingly."

The sound he emitted was more of a cackle than a laugh. He gestured with his gun to a taller man standing by the front door. "Owen, get her out of my way."

In compliance, the man he'd called Owen grabbed Adeline's arms and yanked her off her father. He pinned her arms to her chest, but she kicked hard and connected with his shin. When he still didn't drop her, she bit his forearm. He loosened his grip slightly and she squirmed away, pulling the man's Colt from his holster. Standing between her father and the shorter bearded man, who was obviously the leader, she raised the gun. Before she could shoot, the tall man pushed her and the gun discharged, grazing the shorter man's left arm.

The leader grabbed her with his uninjured arm and crushed her close to his body, pinning her in place with his considerable strength. "You idiot! You got me shot," he shrieked at the other bandit.

"I didn't want you to kill the woman."

"Why the blazes not?"

Owen stared at his feet.

Adeline was forcibly dragged toward the door. "Kill him. Then grab the cash from the safe. It will be my pleasure to prolong the girl's suffering." He traced the outline of her jaw with his handgun. "Finish the job quickly. We need to escape before someone comes calling."

At the sound of another gunshot, the fight drained from Adeline and she allowed herself to be taken captive.

Adeline fought the ropes her captors had tied around her wrists and ankles, but it was no use. It wasn't the first time they'd left her alone for more than a day without access to food or water. It was only a matter of time until she perished from the deplorable conditions she'd been kept in. A sound outside alerted her to their return. She stopped struggling, they would untie her now.

A man she hadn't seen before opened the stall door. "Adeline McCarty?"

At her nod, the man continued, "I'm George Nelson. The Pinkerton Agency has been hired to locate you and ensure your safe return."

Dehydration made speaking nearly impossible, so she nodded. The man took out a knife and cut her bindings.

He gave her his canteen to drink, and then helped her to stand. "Do you think you're strong enough to ride with me to town?"

"I think so."

An hour later they sat at a table in a saloon. She picked at the food he ordered. Hunger gnawed at her, but her stomach was unsettled from drinking too much water too quickly.

"Miss McCarty, this is going to seem odd given the circumstances, but I have a proposition for you."

She raised an eyebrow, but said nothing.

"You may have heard of the Pinkerton Agency before."

"I have. My father has employed your agency many times to investigate railroad crimes."

"Yes, we do a fair amount of work with the railroads."

"Who hired you to find me?"

"Your betrothed."

"I'm not engaged."

"My apologies, but we were led to believe you were by Mr. Cleveland."

"Yes, well I refused his proposals of marriage, but I am grateful he hired you to locate me."

"Are you aware that we have several female detectives on staff?"

"I've heard."

"I know this is too much to ask, and I should refrain myself, but I was wondering."

"What were you wondering, Mr. Nelson?"

"I was wondering if you might be willing to try to get close to your captors. Get them to trust you. If you could do that, you could help save lives."

"Couldn't you lie in wait and ambush them when they come back to camp?"

"We could try, but we'd never get all of them. They have more than one camp and if we don't have proof of their nefarious deeds, we would have to release them."

"How would I get proof?"

"You would observe their doings and send us telegrams

whenever a plan was afoot. Your efforts would make it possible for us to catch them during the commission of a crime."

"How would I accomplish this objective? They keep me tied up. My conditions are worse than that of a common hog."

"I think if you were to make them believe you had accepted your station with them, they might let down their guard around you. You wouldn't be able to make any escape attempts. You'd have to make them believe you enjoyed, or at least tolerated, their company. Once they developed a trust in you, you'd be a valuable asset to the agency."

"I don't see how it would ever work."

"We've done this before and it has worked. Would you be willing to give it a try? We'll keep a detective posted nearby to watch you and make sure you remain unharmed."

Adeline took a deep breath to steady her nerves. She wanted nothing more than to go back to Kansas City and get away from the miscreants who'd taken her captive, but seeing them pay for what they'd done would help ease some of her pain. "They killed my father. I'll do anything I can to bring them to justice."

"You will be well compensated for your effort, Miss McCarty. I appreciate you joining our team."

An hour later, Adeline was back at the camp, bound in her

stall awaiting the return of her captors.

Nate swiped his sleeve across his brow. Hitching his horse, Sunfire, out front, he sauntered into the hotel's saloon keeping his hat pulled low to cover his eyes. It was time to dismantle the Glenn-Ricketts gang and bring Owen Glenn and Ellis Ricketts to justice. Rumor had it they were hiding in Cimarron.

Sidling up to the bar, he ordered a whiskey. He held the devil's drink in his hands, but didn't raise it to his lips. It was part of his cover. It wouldn't do to be conspicuous. Glancing at his pocket watch, he took notice that it was nearly one o'clock, a few drunks sat at the bar and a handful of patrons enjoyed a midday meal. His quarry wasn't in sight. He set his drink on the bar and headed to a nearby boarding house to secure a room away from the action. He didn't need to be kept awake by inebriated men playing late night card games. A decent night's sleep would keep him functioning in top form.

Back at the boarding house, a boy was sent to fill the water trough and get Sunfire some hay. With his horse tended to, Nate ambled inside and stretched out to get some rest. When he awoke at seven that evening, he jumped up and glanced out the window. The sun would be setting soon. He stuffed a sack of coins and his canteen into his bag before putting on his holster.

The ride back to the hotel was pleasantly cool. The blazing sunset lit the sky orange and red as the sun slowly hid itself behind the Sangre de Cristo Mountains.

As he neared the St. James he spotted his quarry. His hand went to the peacemaker on his side. Ellis Ricketts was leaning against a rail near the rear of the building with a comely woman at his side. The woman had auburn curls nearly reaching her waist. She wore no head covering. Her fashionable dress was dirty, torn, and tattered. Something seemed familiar about her. Suddenly, it hit him, there was a bounty out on a fair woman seen with the Glenn-Ricketts gang. She'd taken part in the train robbery in Santa Fe. Most passengers had only been robbed of their valuables, but two former union soldiers had been shot dead. The gang was rumored to have an affiliation with Confederate Bushwhackers. Some claimed the woman was the shooter. He glanced away, not wanting to alert them to his interest.

Bringing his horse around to the front of the hotel, he dismounted and hitched her up before cutting through the establishment. When he neared the rear exit, he slid his Colt .45 from its holster. Leading with his gun, he peered out the door. A cloud of dust greeted him. He managed to get off a couple of shots as the fugitives flew past him on their horses. If only he'd remained with Sunfire, he might've been able to give chase. His quarter horse was fast, but they had a sizable lead. And now the bandits knew they had company. He hurried back to his mare and hoisted himself into the saddle. He would follow the dust trail and see if he could get an idea of where they might be hiding out.

Nate sat at a corner table devouring his food as he surveyed the room. The darkness had made following the fugitives nearly impossible, so he'd come back to the saloon hoping to catch snippets of conversation that might lead him to where the Glenn-Ricketts gang had holed-up.

It was nearing two o'clock in the morning when his patience finally paid-off. A loud drunkard playing cards at a corner table gave him the clue he'd hoped to receive. He headed back to the boarding house to devise a plan of action.

The following morning, Nate dismounted his horse at the St. James Hotel and left her hitched there. Walking the short distance to the Aztec Mill, he pondered his plan of attack. As he crept closer, he kept his right hand on his Colt. Edging his way around the building, he listened intently. Nothing appeared out of the ordinary. Some workers milled around outside, but nothing unusual caught his eye. If the gang had been here, they were long gone.

If the drunkard was to be believed there was suspicious ac-

tivity near Cimarron Canyon. It was about time he headed out there
to investigate. He circled around and back to his mare. Urging Sunfire west, he headed toward the Pallisade Sill.

After riding until noon, he stopped along the riverbank to let
his horse drink and graze. He'd learned in his youth to treat his
horse well, so when the work was grueling, she'd be there for him.
He took some elk jerky from his pack and chewed it while he filled
his canteen. There was still a ways to go and it would be approach-
ing dark by the time he arrived at the Canyon base, so he would
need to set up camp as soon as he reached the Pallisades.

Four hours later he approached the cliffs of the Pallisade
Sill. It was magnificent to behold the Lord's handiwork. When he
reached the base he could no longer see to the top. The sheer magni-
tude of the place awed him. He searched for a decent cleft in the
rock where he could set up camp keeping both himself and Sunfire
out of sight. It took some time, but he found the ideal location before the cool of the evening descended.

As the sun set he walked to the river to fill his canteen. As
he leaned over the river a sharp pain sliced through his skull. He
fought to stay conscious and he turned to face his attacker. A vision
with waist-length auburn locks tossed a large rock aside. Nate's

senses slowly came back to him and he wrestled the vicious woman to the ground. When he had her arms twisted behind her back so she couldn't do him any more harm, the little vixen started kicking. A blow to his shin sent him stumbling back. He reached out and took hold of her wrists again and handcuffed her.

"What do you think you're doing, Miss?" He held her still.

"Protecting myself."

"From what? A man getting a drink of water?"

"From a man intruding on a woman's private washing time."

"Well, excuse me. How was I to know you were here washing?"

"You're going to pretend you innocently stumbled down here? These cliffs go for miles and miles, yet you just happened to come to my bathing hole for a drink of water."

"I had no idea you were here. I didn't even see you until after you'd hit me in the head with a rock."

"I'm sorry I hit you. Would you kindly remove the handcuffs?"

"No."

"Why not?"

"Because I'm a bounty hunter. As delightful company as I'm sure you'll make, you are a woman wanted for murder, so I'll have to put up with you."

"Murder? I've never harmed anyone in my life."

"Seems you and the law have differing opinions, honey. I'm taking you in. You can sort it out with the sheriff."

"So you lied? You knew I was here?"

"I'd heard your gang was holed-up in these cliffs. I did not know you were bathing in this part of the river at the exact moment I was getting a drink. I did not lie."

"I don't believe you."

"Believe what you like. I imagine if we head out in the morning, I can have you back to Santa Fe in three or four days and you'll be hanged by the weekend. You'll no longer be my problem." He pushed her along in front of him toward his campsite.

"You won't get away with this. They'll come looking for me."

"I hope they come to get you. The bounty on the men is twice what I'll get for you. I'd take pleasure to taking them in. Maybe even bring you to the local sheriff in Cimarron before we head to Santa Fe. He'd love bragging rights for taking part in bringing down the Glenn-Ricketts Gang."

Adeline shivered.

The bounty hunter came closer. Too close. "You're cold."

She gazed at the sky.

"Let me help you move closer to the fire."

"I don't need your help."

"If I take these cuffs off, will you behave yourself? I don't want to have to shoot a woman."

Adeline didn't want to be agreeable with the man who intended to see her hang, but the pain in her wrists won out. She nodded. There was no reason to suffer more than necessary.

He moved her hair over her shoulder. "Your hair is wet. Dry it by the fire." She was unable to control the jolt of pleasure she felt when he touched her. He helped her up, removed the cuffs and settled her on a rock near the fire."

"Thank you." It pained her to utter the polite words.

"What's your name?"

"Shouldn't you know it?"

"I should. I don't."

"How can you bring in a bounty when you don't know who you're hunting?"

"I knew who I was hunting. Glenn and Ricketts. I'd seen your wanted poster, but didn't notice the name. You weren't my target until you decided to smash me over the head with a rock."

"What makes you think I'm the woman from the poster?"

"Your extraordinary beauty caught my eye. It's not often you come across a captivating criminal."

"Flattery will get you nowhere."

"When I saw you in town with Ricketts, he seemed to be getting somewhere."

Her hands itched to reach out and slap him. "You're mistaken." More like ignorant and uninformed.

"Behind the St. James. The two of you seemed awfully cozy."

"You shot at us! That was you."

"It was, but you temporarily eluded me."

"You shot at me."

"I was shooting at Ricketts. You happened to be in the way."

"Would you shoot anyone who was in the way?"

"Only if they were a fellow miscreant." He stretched out.

She lifted her chin. "My name is Adeline."

He smiled. "I'm Nathaniel Hayes." The firelight danced in his cornflower blue eyes.

"Aren't you concerned the fire will draw unwanted attention?"

"I was hoping it might bring your friends in."

Ever the man hunter. She wondered if he ever relaxed. "May I ask you something?"

"I'm listening."

"Do you truly want to see a woman hang?"

"No."

"Then why are you bringing me in?"

"It's not up to me to decide your fate."

"It is up to you. You arrested me. You can let me go."

"Maybe so, but I take my responsibility seriously. I pledged to uphold the law."

"You'll let an innocent woman hang?"

"You didn't look innocent when I saw you with Ricketts, honey."

"Don't call me 'honey'. We've established my name is Adeline."

"It's time to get some rest, honey. We ride out first thing in the morning." He led her to a cleft in the foot of the rocky cliff.

She glanced around the dark enclosure. Her heart raced and her stomach flipped as panic gripped her.

"You can use my bedroll. I'll sleep on the other side."

She took a deep breath and forced herself to relax when she realized he didn't plan to take liberties with her.

He held out the handcuffs. "Get comfortable before I reattach these."

"Do you have to put them back on?"

"I do. You cannot be trusted."

Adeline lay awake as the bounty hunter snored beside her. He'd kept a respectful distance. She appreciated that. The past five months had taught her more about human depravity than she should've learned in a lifetime. She didn't intend to stick around and wait for the attractive lawkeeper to take her to the sheriff. She shivered. There was no telling if it was from the chill in the night air or the dread of being led to the gallows.

There would be no witnesses on her behalf at the mock trial they would hold. They wouldn't let her send a telegram to the Pinkerton Agency. No. Her only chance of survival was escape.

She was befuddled as to how they'd come to believe her guilty of murder. The train robbery had been a disaster, but she'd tried to stop the shooting. She'd placed herself between Ellis Ricketts and his victims, but all she accomplished was earning herself a brutal beating. Ellis had a vicious temper.

After finally managing to remove a hairpin from her dress pocket, she maneuvered the best she could to get an angle that would allow her to pick the lock on the handcuffs. At the click of the handcuffs releasing, she glanced in the direction of the man sleeping six feet away. She remained still until she was sure he hadn't stirred. Even with his face obscured by shadows, she could picture every detail of his face from his strong jaw to the dimples that appeared when he smiled. She wondered how he got the scar under his left eye. Rubbing her sore wrists, she quietly rose to her feet. Her dress and petticoats seemed to make an inordinate amount of noise. She held them tightly to her legs, to keep them as quiet as possible while she snuck away from the rock enclosure. Moments later she stood beside the bounty hunter's quarter horse. She took a minute to introduce herself to the chestnut mare before saddling her. It wouldn't do well to spook her. Mounting the good-natured beast she took off toward town, urging the horse into a gallop. If she did-n't get a message to the agency soon, she would die for a crime she hadn't committed.

An hour later, Adeline slowed the horse to a more comforta-ble walk.

She stroked the horse's long neck. "Thank you, sweet girl. You saved my life back there. If I hadn't been able to get away quickly your master would've delivered me to the gallows."

Chapter 2

Nate woke with a start. Thick darkness surrounded him, but he sensed something off. Then he remembered the woman. Rolling off his makeshift bed he leaned over to check on her. She was gone. He didn't need to check to know Sunfire would be missing. How had he been so foolish?

It didn't take much time to pack his supplies. With no horse to load he was in for a challenge. Might as well finish the job he came here for. The Glenn-Ricketts boys were in this canyon. The woman might've warned them off, but they couldn't have packed camp so quickly. If he could locate their hide-out, he'd find his horse and apprehend the fugitives before daybreak.

Once the sun rose the heat was brutal. The methodical search was turning up nothing. Three hours into the search he finally located people. He'd been checking behind a rock which jutted out from the cliff when he heard voices. From what he could tell there were several of them. Peeking past the wall of stone he took inventory of the situation. It appeared as if there were five fugitives. They were arguing. A lanky man with chin-length hair pulled a revolver from his holster, but he was dead before he could raise it enough to fire. It was one way to solve a disagreement, but certainly not a smart one.

The men went back to discussing their plans. Nate wished he could make out their exact words. He caught snippets of the conversation, but not enough to determine where they were going. When they split up, he hung back until they were out of sight and followed the path of two of the bandits. They were headed away from where he'd already searched, so he figured they might lead him back to their camp. Ten minutes later, he heard the neighing of horses, and found the camp.

Cautiously entering the camp, thankful he had two revolvers, he raised both guns and pointed them at the men's heads. Cocking them both.

"What the—."

"Put your hands up or I'll shoot." The men glanced over their shoulders, and the one of the left must've decided odds were not in his favor despite it being two against one. He slowly raised his hands and, following a brief hesitation, his cohort did the same. Nate reached for handcuffs and the bandit on the right drew on him. It was a clean shot to the heart. Ellis Ricketts had taken his last breath.

Nate took a deep breath and raised an eyebrow. "You want to try me too?"

"No."

"Good. Turn around. I'm going to cuff you."

Once Nate had the man cuffed, he walked him to the horses. "You got a name?"

"John Bradshaw."

"Well, John, I don't think there's a bounty on your head, but I'm taking you in anyway."

Bradshaw gave a curt nod.

"Where's my horse?" Nate asked.

"Your horse?"

"The one the woman stole?"

"What woman? Adeline? She's been gone since last evening."

"So, she didn't show up here this morning?"

"No. Ellis thought she'd run off. He was fixing to give her

another beating when he caught up to her."

"A gentleman through and through."

It took a great deal of effort to lift Ellis onto the horse and tie him down. Nate tied the reins from one of the horses over the saddle horn of the lead horse. He helped John to mount the horse before hoisting himself up and leading the way. As much as he wanted to catch up with Owen Glenn, now wouldn't be the best time. The exhaustion of the morning's search and the afternoon's labors were catching up with him. Besides, he needed to find Adeline and retrieve Sunfire.

Nate stopped to let the horses rest. He'd have preferred to push on, but with unfamiliar horses and a prisoner, it was best to stop. In another two hours they'd make it back into town. He filled his canteen and gave it to John to drink.

"So what is the woman's story? How'd she wind up with your gang?"

"It's not my gang."

"Tell me about the girl."

"Adeline?"

"Is there another female hanging around?"

"Not that I've seen. From what I hear they snatched her in Kansas City when she attempted to save her daddy's life. Brave little woman. Got between Ellis and her daddy. Lucky she didn't take a bullet for him."

The man took another drink of water before continuing. "Ellis told Owen to put a bullet through the man's heart. I'm surprised Owen could do it. He's not real keen on shooting people."

"No? How'd he end up leading a gang?"

"He doesn't lead anything. He's Ellis' puppet."

"Is that so?"

"Absolutely."

"So, when did Adeline turn bad?"

"Ada? Turn bad? Didn't happen. She may have Ellis and Owen hoodwinked, but I see through her facade."

"How's that?"

"When they first brought her to the campsite, back in Albuquerque, we kept her locked in a horse stall. Then suddenly she stops misbehaving. Next thing you know Ellis gives her a little freedom. The woman has been patiently planning her escape. I'd have helped her, too. If she asked."

"What makes you so sure she planned to leave? How do you know she's not in cahoots with Ellis?"

"I see her face when she thinks no one is looking. That woman is full of hatred. She's been plotting her escape and ultimately her revenge."

"If that's true, why'd she participate in the train robbery?"

"Ada? Participate? She was there for certain, but her only involvement was the beating she got for getting in the way when Ellis first tried to shoot those traitorous yanks."

"Traitorous yanks?"

"Them brothers Ellis shot were killers in the war. They were bragging about it."

"They were bragging while you were in the middle of robbing them?"

"Oh no. Ellis' heard 'em bragging one night at a saloon in Kansas City some time ago. It was good fortune they was on that train."

"Huh? So you mean to tell me Adeline didn't shoot anyone and she wasn't complicit in the robbery?"

"That little woman wouldn't shoot a man, except maybe Ellis, but it's too late for her to do that now."

"Why not Owen if he killed her dad?"

"She knows it wasn't his decision. I don't think she'd take revenge on him."

"There's a bounty out on her. I hope I get to her before the law or another bounty hunter does."

"Good luck. She's probably long gone by now."

"Maybe."

Adeline smoothed her hair the best she could. She stared at the picture of herself hanging outside the telegraph office. Was there any chance she wouldn't be recognized? If only she had a hat to hide herself some. It was time to notify the Pinkerton Agency of her predicament. With any luck they would inform the sheriff she was an undercover detective working for them before they had a chance to deliver their own form of justice. She wanted to go home. Not that there was anything left for her there. Maria had probably found new employment it had been months. She would've taken the rest of the staff with her, or found them other work. Without her father, there was nothing.

She squared her shoulders and did her best to appear casual as she entered the telegraph office. "I need to send a telegram please."

SIR. STOP

TROUBLE. STOP

NEED PROOF I'M DETECTIVE. STOP

NOTIFY SHERIFF.

A.M.

She paid with money she'd stolen from the bounty hunter. What else could she do? It was imperative she get a message to Mr. Pinkerton if she was to avoid hanging. Now she had to find some place to lay low. The saloon was an option, but one she detested. Glancing around, she spotted the church. It was as good a place as any to hide herself for a time. Heading inside she ducked into a pew. Being inside the church kindled a desire to pray in Adeline. Prayer no longer came easily. It wasn't that she didn't believe God was there, but she had so many questions He wasn't answering. Why would He allow her father to be murdered? Why would He allow her to be kidnapped? Why would He allow her to be whipped and beaten? Her father's devotion to God seemed to have been strengthened by the loss of her mother. He had a powerful faith she didn't understand. Her own faith felt like it was slipping away.

She dropped to her knees and bowed her head. Only a few words came, but she knew God could read her heart, so she lifted herself to Him and surrendered her own will, asking Him to heal her battered heart. Adeline felt her eyes beginning to close. Not getting any sleep the previous night was catching up to her.

She startled at the hand on her shoulder. Jumping to her feet she slammed her hip into the pew. "Not you again."

The man had the gall to chuckle. "Sorry, but yes. Me again. You left my horse outside. You must've wanted to be found."

"I didn't think you'd get back to town so fast without your horse."

"I've already been to the sheriff. Dropped off John Bradshaw."

"You captured John?"

"I did. He had some interesting tales to tell."

"He's a criminal. You can't believe anything he tells you."

"Oh no? So, I shouldn't believe you're innocent? That you had nothing to do with the train robbery and murders?"

"That you can believe."

"I could get a decent bounty on you, but I don't need the money. Ellis Ricketts' corpse is worth more than enough to keep me comfortable for some time."

Relief spread through her at his words. "Ellis is dead?"

"He is. There's a problem though. There are wanted posters hanging around town. So, if I leave you here, someone is going to turn you in. You can ride with me and I'll keep you safe until your name can be cleared."

"I have someone working on that already."

"What are you going to do in the meantime? The gallows wait for no man. Or woman."

"They'll send a telegram letting everyone know I'm innocent."

"Who are they?"

"The Pinkerton Agency."

"I'm confused."

"A former suitor paid the Pinkerton Agency to rescue me. Instead of rescuing me, they recruited me."

"A lady detective? You're joking?"

"Of course not. They hired the first female detective nearly twenty-seven years ago. It's not new."

"It's new to me. What did they ask you to do?"

"Remain with the gang and pretend to comply with their demands. They wanted me to see if I could befriend them to get information."

"You agreed to do this? To stay with a group of bandits?"

"I wanted to help bring them to justice. I've been sending

the agency information whenever I can sneak away for a few minutes to send a telegram. Mr. Pinkerton had an agent keeping watch on me. The first couple of weeks he stopped by and helped me when they would leave me locked up. I would tell him what I knew and he would leave again before they returned, but I haven't seen him in weeks. Maybe something bad happened to him."

"You mentioned a suitor? Are you to be married?"

"Our fathers had hoped so, but I had no interest. I don't think he did either."

"Come with me. I'll keep you safe."

"I can take care of myself."

Nate moved closer to her, so that he towered over her. "You made your self-reliance abundantly clear when you smashed me in the head with that rock, and again when you broke free and ran off in the middle of the night. It was the first time I'd lost a captive. However, here in town your chances aren't nearly as good as they were back at that canyon."

Adeline glared at him. "I'll get out of town. I'll return after Mr. Pinkerton has a chance to fix things."

"And when do you think that will be? A week? Two?"

"No more than a day."

"You have quite a bit of faith in your boss."

"I do."

"I hope he comes through for you. I'm heading out. I have a corpse to deliver. Godspeed."

"Farewell."

"I'm taking my horse."

"What am I going to do with no money and no horse?"

"No money?" He chuckled. "You're a smart woman. I guess you'll figure it out."

Nate laughed to himself as Adeline rushed out the church doors behind him. He'd assumed she would follow. Only insanity would cause a woman to willingly remain stranded in Cimarron without a horse. He'd left two of the horses with the sheriff and Ricketts' corpse was still slung over a horse. Nate didn't want the hassle of taking the extra horse along, but he didn't want to share his horse with the dead man either. He'd have preferred bringing him in alive, but at least dead men didn't make a fuss.

"So, Adeline, where are you from?"

"Kansas City."

"According to John Bradshaw, your trip out here wasn't

particularly pleasant."

"An understatement. They murdered my father and dragged me from the only home I'd ever known."

"Sorry. I shouldn't have brought up the subject. I'm not adept at small talk."

"And why is that, Mr. Bounty Hunter?"

"I'm a bit of a loner."

She batted her eyelashes teasingly. "Is there no Mistress Bounty Hunter waiting at home for you?"

"I'm afraid not. Most folks call me Nate, not Mr. Bounty Hunter."

"People call me Addy, but I can't say I like it much."

"If that's the case, I'll continue to address you as Adeline."

The woman was beautiful. She was dusty, dirty, and her hair was a tangled mess, but she was still attractive. They weren't too far from his father's ranch. They could go there and she could get herself cleaned up. He might even leave her at the ranch while he delivered Ricketts to Santa Fe. It would give the Pinkertons time to clear things up.

About three hours later they arrived at the ranch.

"What are we doing here?"

"I thought you might want the chance to get cleaned up. We can lay low here for a while and give the Pinkertons a chance to prove your innocence."

"Where are we?"

"My dad's ranch."

"He won't mind?"

"Not one bit. He enjoys the company of a pretty woman as much as I do."

Nate jumped off the horse and greeted his father as he rushed toward them.

"Pa, I want you to meet Adeline." Nate and his father walked back over to the horses and Nate helped Adeline dismount.

"Pleasure to meet you, sir."

"The name is Timothy Hayes." Nathaniel's father headed for the door. "Let's not stand around out here lollygagging. Son, drag the corpse into the shed, don't need it out baking in the sun."

Nate wrestled the body down off the horse.

"When you're done, Nate, tend to the horses." His father turned toward Adeline "Adeline, you come on in and get a bite to eat."

"I can help with the horses."

"Nonsense. Come on now."

Adeline glanced helplessly at Nate. He shrugged and dragged the body toward the shed.

Nate's father set a sizable helping of pork and beans in front of Adeline. "Thank you, Mr. Hayes."

"You can call me Timothy, if you like."

"I'll stick with Mr. Hayes. Timothy sounds disrespectful."

"Nonsense. But you do as you like. Shall we pray so you can get to eating?"

"Shouldn't we wait for Nathaniel?"

"Not if you're hungry."

"I can wait a few minutes."

"Well, if you're not going to eat, tell me about yourself."

"Not much to tell. I was born in Philadelphia, but my father moved us to Kansas City. He was a business man. Worked with the railroad."

"What about your Ma?"

"I don't remember her. She passed when I was a child.

Pneumonia."

"I'm sorry to hear that. Nate lost his mother to sickness too. She died of cholera."

"I'm sorry for your loss, sir."

"It was a long time ago and she's with the Lord. I'll see her again."

"That's a pleasant way to look at it."

"It's the only way to look at it as far as I'm concerned. It's the truth. Here comes my boy now. Nate, are you hungry? Adeline wouldn't start eating without you."

"I'm famished." Nate sat at the kitchen table and his father dished him up some pork. "Thanks, Pa."

"Enjoy it."

The two men were remarkably similar in appearance. The father had a few more lines around his mouth and eyes, but the resemblance was unmistakable.

Adeline watched them interact, enjoying their entertaining banter.

"Have you heard from Isaiah?" Nate asked.

"Not in the past few weeks."

"Maybe he'll send word soon."

"I'm sure he will. I'm going to go find Rosa. She can fix a room for you, Adeline. Then she'll take you to the creek, so you can get washed up. The creek is cold, but bearable this time of year."

"That sounds delightful. Thank you, Mr. Hayes."

"Who is Isaiah?"

"My little brother. He was itching to get off the ranch. As soon as he was old enough, he moved to Texas. A few months ago, he joined the rangers."

"I hope he'll stay safe."

"Me too."

She spotted Rosa standing off to the side, unobtrusively, so she joined her. The Housekeeper, a kindly older woman with a heavy Spanish accent reminded her of Maria. Maria was likely beside herself with worry. She'd assumed Maria had moved on to new employment, but what if she hadn't. Guilt gnawed at Adeline's stomach. She should've made contact with home.

Adeline joined Nate on the screen porch, sitting in the rocking chair farthest from him. He watched as she finger combed her long strands of red hair.

"I trust you feel better after bathing."

"Much. Thank you."

"I'm glad Rosa had a dress for you to wear."

"It's slightly big, but it will allow me to clean and mend my own dress."

"Did you get along well with Rosa?" He stood.

"Doesn't everyone?"

"If she doesn't like a person, she's obvious about it."

"Then she must've liked me, as she was kind and helpful."

"Glad to hear it." He held his hand out to her. "Would you care to take a stroll with me, Adeline?"

"That would be acceptable." She let him help her up.

They walked along a dirt path.

"What do you think of the ranch?"

"It's beautiful. I'm not sure I've ever seen so many cattle."

"Pa built himself a nice life here."

"Why don't you work as a cattleman?"

"Pa wants me here, but I wasn't skilled at following directions. I can't work for another man."

"Not even your Pa?"

"I couldn't when I was younger, but I'm not the same man I was at the time. Maybe, I could now. But why change what's working? I like what I do."

"It's dangerous work."

"You don't think working with a ton of bull is dangerous?"

"Of course it is, but it's not the same as getting shot at."

"No. That it isn't." They walked in silence for several minutes before he continued. "What about you? When this is over are you going to go back to a quiet life in Kansas City, or do you intend to continue on as a Pinkerton detective?"

"There's nothing left for me at home. I may give this detective thing a chance."

"You realize detective work is dangerous?"

"I certainly do."

"Why risk it?"

"If I can help one person avoid the pain I endured these last months, it will be worth the risk."

They neared the creek, so Nate held his hand out to Adeline to help her navigate the rocks safely. He wasn't prepared for the jolt he felt at the simple touch. When they reached the other side, he reluctantly released her. His eyes searched hers for a sign she'd felt something too, but he couldn't be sure. It didn't matter anyway. He could see no future for them.

Adeline walked to the back of the wrap-around porch and pulled the lightweight shawl tightly around her against the cool of the night. The moon was barely a sliver, but she could see the faint outline of the outbuildings. Maybe she could convince Nathaniel to take her to the stables in the morning. She might even be able to help out with the work. Growing up with servants, she didn't have much experience with manual labor, but she would like to learn more about the workings of the ranch.

Hearing footsteps behind her, she jumped. "Adeline, are you having trouble sleeping?"

She relaxed at the sound of his voice. "I haven't tried to sleep. I'm still wound up from the day's adventures."

He approached closely behind her and moved the hair from off her neck. "You're finally safe. You should sleep."

"I'm not sure how safe I am with you so close."

"I won't hurt you, Adeline."

She considered the words. He wouldn't hurt her intentionally, but she was convinced if she let him get close, he would crush her heart. It would be best not to let him in. "I trust you believe that, Nathaniel."

He rested his hands on her shoulders and took a step closer.

"It's the truth."

She was pinned between him and the railing, but she had no desire to escape. Turning, she gazed into his eyes, but they were shrouded in darkness. "I want to believe you."

His thumb traced the line of her jaw and her insides did a little flip.

Abruptly, he stepped away. "You should get some rest. It's been some time since you were able to sleep in relative safety."

Safety. She was certain she was not safe as long as she was under the same roof as Nathaniel Hayes.

He laced his fingers through hers and led her back inside the house. When they reached the steps, he released her. "Goodnight, Adeline."

"Goodnight."

It was a great effort to keep her steps slow. She wanted to run to the room she'd been assigned and close the door. Yet, she knew it was futile. There was no escaping the feelings Nathaniel had evoked in such a short time.

Once in bed, she snuggled under the coverlet and tried to force images of his crystal blue eyes and strong, gentle hands from her thoughts. Instead she imagined what it would be like to feel his lips on hers.

Chapter 3

Nate prepared the horses for the journey before going inside to let Adeline know he was leaving.

She didn't answer when he knocked on the bedroom door. Opening the door, he stood there in the doorway and stared at the sleeping woman. Guilt gnawed at his gut. He shouldn't have entered her room.

Adeline sat straight up, eyes wide open.

"I'm sorry, I shouldn't have come in, but you didn't hear me knocking."

"Sleeping in a camp of bandits, I haven't managed a full night's sleep in ages. I guess I needed it."

"I'm going to be gone for a couple of days. You're in good hands with Pa."

She scrambled to get out of bed, leaving him a view of criss-crossed scars. She must've remembered her state of undress, because she stopped and pulled the blanket up. "You shouldn't be in here."

He turned away. "I know. I'm going." The scars he'd glimpsed burned themselves into his consciousness.

Adeline must have dressed in record time because she was already on his heels as he approached the horses. "You're not leaving me behind."

He tightened the saddle on his horse. "I'm trying to keep your pretty head attached to your lovely neck."

"And I'm supposed to sit around here and do nothing all day?"

She batted her eyelashes in mock flirtation.

"I'm inured to your charms, love." He mounted the horse. "You can help Rosa cook and clean. Bradshaw tells me you're competent with domestic tasks."

The flash of annoyance that lit her eyes gave him a strange satisfaction. At a touch of his calves, Sunfire left Adeline standing in a cloud of dust. Nate glanced back at her and grinned.

Riding to Santa Fe was an adventure he usually enjoyed. Solitude was something he'd learned to embrace. Precious hours spent with only God for company. This time his thoughts were consumed with the captivating maiden he'd left back at the ranch. He thought about the adorable sprinkling of freckles across the bridge of her nose, how the sunlight brought out golden highlights in her auburn hair, and how she wrinkled her forehead and bit her lip when she was frustrated. And he thought about how he couldn't keep his hands to himself. He'd be best off keeping some distance between them. And his errant thoughts were all the proof he needed. He'd never spent his rides daydreaming about a woman before. Life alone suited him fine. Until now.

When he finally rode into town the following day, he'd come to the realization he had to get Adeline's dilemma resolved because if he didn't get her out of his life now, he'd not soon be able to forget her.

The general store was open when he arrived. He asked the woman behind the counter to assist him in collecting the essentials a woman about her size and age would need. The woman discreetly gathered together items he wouldn't have thought to purchase. She added some sweet-smelling soap, perfume, and a reticule to the counter.

"What about a dress and a hat?" he asked.

"We don't have much selection here, but I'll give you what I have. She'll need to be measured, so we can make her a beautiful dress."

"Please give me what you have for now and I will bring her in when it's convenient."

The woman disappeared into the back and came back with a lovely mint green dress with a matching hat.

Nate paid for his purchases. "Thank you, Miss. You've been most helpful." He stowed the packages on his horse and took off toward the sheriff's office.

He sauntered in and held out his hand in greeting. "Brought you a cold one, Harry."

The sheriff shook the proffered hand with unnecessary strength. "Who'd you bring in this time?" The sheriff tried to look past him.

"Come on out and see. I must warn you, he's not looking too good. It's been a few days."

"We can live with dead as long as he's still recognizable." The sheriff lifted the blanket from the corpse. "You brought me Ellis Ricketts?"

"I did. The fool drew on me."

"A mistake he didn't live to regret, I see."

"I reckon not."

"Well, I owe you some money. Let's get that taken care of." They walked inside and the sheriff took money from the safe, giving it to Nate. "You able to stick around and help me bury this low-down scoundrel before he stinks up the whole town?"

"Sure. Least I can do for failing to bring him in alive."

"You're about the only man hunter I work with who would care if you brought him in dead or alive."

"The smell is a good enough reason to bring them in kicking, but I don't like having a man's death on my conscious. It especially goads when I doubt they've ever been right with their maker."

"I can see how that would haunt a man."

They buried the bandit in an unmarked grave in an area of the cemetery reserved for unknowns and criminals. Sheriff Moore slapped Nate's back "How about joining me for a scotch?"

"No thanks. You know I'm not a drinker. Besides, I want to get a couple of hours of riding in before stopping for the night."

"Suit yourself. I'm gonna go celebrate with the townsfolk."

"You sure you wouldn't rather go home and celebrate with Mary."

"I think I'll take her out with me to celebrate."

"Good idea."

"Who are you chasing after next?"

"Owen Glenn."

"What about the lady they had with them? No sign of her?"

Nate's back stiffened. "One of Rickett's cohorts claims she was innocent."

"I guess the law will make a determination, won't it?"

"I suppose so." He skirted the issue. "John Bradshaw was the accomplice. He didn't have a bounty, so I left him with the sheriff in Cimarron."

"Wish you'd have brought him here. I would've liked to take a crack at questioning him."

"Sorry."

"I wonder if Joe will send him here."

"Send him a telegram. He might."

"Hopefully, you'll find the woman when you get Owen Glenn."

The hair on Nate's neck stood at attention. "I'll be seeing you, Harry."

"Take care, Nate. These dubious men you chase are dangerous."

"Don't I know it?"

"Ever think of settling down? Taking a local job?"

"I haven't. No." Nate raised a hand in a half-hearted wave as he made his way back to his horse.

Adeline hadn't found much to keep her occupied in the long two days Nate had been away. She'd been helping the housekeeper with mundane tasks, but it wasn't occupying her mind. It bothered her to be doing exactly what Nathaniel expected of her. He'd said as much. Clearly he didn't know a thing about her. She'd been raised the pampered daughter of a wealthy man.

Nathaniel implied she should be keeping house. If he knew who her father was, he wouldn't treat her like his servant girl. Her upbringing no longer mattered now, did it? Daddy was gone and she'd get a fine inheritance, but once she married, if she married, it would go to her husband. And he could do with it as he pleased. It rankled, but she would come to accept it. Maybe she'd stay single. Nathaniel was pleasant to look upon, but he wasn't looking for a wife and she wasn't looking for a husband anyway. She inwardly admonished herself for allowing her thoughts to turn to Nathaniel when the thought of marriage arose. Maybe she was more interested in him than she wanted to admit to herself.

Every little noise had her looking for Nathaniel's return.

The ride would be a difficult one. He wouldn't want to over burden his horse with too many hours on the trail, but she couldn't help hoping he'd return soon.

She walked to the bedroom window and stared out over the pastures. Taking in the beauty of the ranch surrounded by mountain peaks, she sighed. God was indeed an artist. The image of Nathaniel's face replaced the view as it filled her thoughts. His face was etched in her mind and in her daydreams she traced the line of his jaw. Why she was fantasizing about him was a mystery. She'd not been given to romantic notions about men in the past.

Was it possible her attraction was linked to his killing Ellis Ricketts? It was awful of her to be happy Ellis was dead, but it was a relief. He'd done terrible things. Her hands automatically felt for her ribs where bruises lingered from her last beating. Yet, despite the deep sense of relief that he couldn't hurt her anymore, she had an overwhelming sense of sadness. A life was lost. Somewhere there was a mother who'd given birth to a baby boy and had hoped for a noble and honorable life for her child. Such a waste. She placed her hand on her own abdomen. Someday she might have the opportunity to have a child. Would he or she live a life pleasing to God? Was *she* living a life pleasing to God? He wouldn't be happy with her rejoicing over a man's death. She was sure of that much.

Getting down on her knees, she prayed, confessed her thoughts and feelings and asked for guidance to help her live a righteous life despite what she'd been through.

Climbing into bed, Adeline pulled the quilt up and prayed some more asking God to bring Nathaniel back safely. She also prayed for her innocence to be proven so she could go home. Yet a nagging feeling told her it wasn't time for her to go home. There was nobody left in Kansas City. What was her home without her father?

After tossing and turning for what felt like hours, she allowed her mind to once again remember the details of Nathaniel's handsome face and broad shoulders. It might be scandalous, but it was nicer to think of him than her father's murder or the deceased miscreant who killed him.

Adeline ran across the yard toward him as Nate hopped off his horse.

"In a hurry to greet me?"

"Do you have any news? Am I free?" It was painful to think she was in such a hurry to leave. He wasn't her suitor. As comely as she was, she was nothing more than a bounty. He'd do well to remember that.

"Not yet. I'm sorry to say." Nate ran his fingers through his hair. "The sheriff wanted me to bring you in. I didn't mention you were already in custody."

"Is that what this is?" She put her hands on her hips. "I'm in custody? You're holding me here for the law?"

"That's not what I meant."

"What did you mean?" She sputtered and took a step back.

He reached out a hand to touch her shoulder, but she pulled away. "I meant I was trying to keep you safe."

"I don't need you to keep me safe." She took another step back.

"Please. Stay here." He threw up his hands. "You're not in custody, but I'd like you to stay."

She turned and stormed off toward the house.

What was he thinking? He should've given her a horse and let her go. It didn't make sense to keep her around when she affected his thoughts and clouded his judgment.

He took care of his horse and put away the tack. Then he led his horse out to the pasture and stood staring out at the herd. Maybe he'd take another horse and get back on the hunt today. There wasn't a lot of point in hanging around the ranch with a seething woman.

His father moseyed up to the fence line where Nate stood

watching the horses.

"Son, what's going on with you and that little filly?"

"I don't know what you're talking about. I told you the situation. She needs my help until her situation is resolved."

"Do you think I'm blind? I can see what's in front of my nose."

Nate narrowed his eyes.

"If your intentions toward her are not honorable than you should ride out again. That girl has been through enough. She doesn't need to have her heart broken."

A muscle in Nate's jaw clenched and unclenched. "I'll ride out in a couple of hours. I have no intention of getting tied to a woman with a man's job."

Nate stalked off toward the house.

Adeline cornered Nate in the stables. "Where are you going this time?"

"To hunt down Owen Glenn."

"You're not leaving me here."

"I don't see any other option."

She put her hands on her hips and glared at him. "I'm coming with you."

"It's not safe."

"I can help."

He removed his hat and swiped at his brow to dry the sweat. "How do you propose to do so when you can't show your face in town?"

"I can camp on the edge of town."

Nate pretended to consider her request. "Let me think about." He scratched the side of his head. "No. You aren't going with me."

"I know where they plan to hit next."

"Then why haven't you filled me in?"

"I thought I might need the leverage later to avoid the gallows."

"I've got to get going."

"You don't want the information?" She blocked his path from the stables by standing in the narrow walkway between the stables and the outer wall.

"Move out of the way."

"Not until you agree to let me come with you."

He got close to her, too close, daring her to remain planted. When she didn't move he got even closer pressing his body against hers. "This is your last chance to get out of my way," he growled.

She peered up at him, something akin to desire burning in her eyes. He allowed himself a moment to consider his options. Her lips parted. He could kiss the willing woman blocking his path or he could do the honorable thing. The temptation nearly overwhelmed him, but in the end his conscience won out. He put his hands on her waist and lifted her, tossing her over his shoulder.

Her fists pounded against his back.

He chuckled as he deposited her on the ground outside of the stables. "Did you expect me to do something improper?" He asked

"Hauling me around like a sack of potatoes is most improper if you ask me."

"It's a good thing nobody is asking you." Nate brushed the hair from her face. He allowed his thumb to trace a trail across her bottom lip, but resisted the urge to lower his mouth to hers and pull her into his arms. "I'll see you in a couple of days, Adeline."

Adeline was not going to sit around the house waiting for

that insufferable man to decide her fate.

She saddled an Arabian gelding. It was mid-afternoon when Cimarron came into view. She'd carefully wound her hair atop her head and covered it with the new hat Nathaniel purchased for her. She tugged the hat down to obscure her features and rode into town on main street.

When she reached the church, she brought the horse to a stop and dismounted. Her legs were stiff and numb from the ride. In an attempt to get the feeling back in her legs, she stomped her feet kicking up dust. She needed to rest and think.

There was a cool breeze in the church when she entered. She sat in the pew she'd occupied on her last visit and considered her options. If she was going to provide proof of her innocence, she'd have to find a way to get one of them to admit it. Bradshaw's comments to Nathaniel would help, but she needed more. To get it, she would have to find Owen. Knowing he intended to rob a Wells-Fargo stage coach before it got into Cimarron was a start, but she didn't know what day it would arrive or where they would intercept it. She'd heard something about a narrow pass, but no specifics. Maybe she was already too late.

The information she needed was unlikely to materialize within the walls of the church. She could ask at the telegraph office, but they might recognize her and she didn't want to spend her night behind bars.

Nate strolled into the sheriff's office.

"Hello, Sheriff."

"Nate. Great to see you. Did you get Ricketts delivered to Santa Fe without complications?"

"Harry roped me into helping him bury the body, but I got my reward."

"What brings you back to Cimarron?"

"I'm tracking Owen Glenn."

"Pleased to hear that," Sheriff Jack Garrison replied.

"I'd like another chance to talk to Bradshaw. May I?"

"I guess you didn't hear?" Jack scratched at his beard. "Bradshaw escaped two nights ago."

"How did he manage that?"

"With help from Owen Glenn and others, I reckon. They nearly destroyed my jail with explosives. Blew the gate clean off. It's a wonder they didn't blow Bradshaw to bits in the process."

"How do you know they didn't?" Nate asked.

"They wouldn't have had the courtesy to remove the corpse."

"I suppose not. I'm going to head over to the saloon and grab a bite to eat. Maybe I'll hear something worth pursuing."

"I'm headed over there myself. I'll only be a moment if you want to wait we can go together."

"You're not much to look at, but I can tolerate your company through one meal," Nate said.

The sheriff laughed.

A few minutes later, they sat and ordered.

"So, Jack. Do you enjoy being a sheriff?"

"That's an odd question."

"It was something Harry said got me thinking. He asked if I'd ever considered a career change."

"I don't think you'll stop hunting men until you're a decrepit old man."

"I do relish the thrill of the hunt."

"I enjoy my work as sheriff. It has it's challenges, certainly." He smirked. "Like having the Glenn-Ricketts boys destroy the jail. It has its rewards, as well."

"What are the rewards?"

"The townsfolk respect me. I get to go home and sleep in my own bed every night. Best of all, the few women we have around here are clamoring for my attentions. I guess lawmen are in high demand."

"Funny you should mention that. I see several of Miss Patty's women looking your way."

"It's more likely they're glancing in your direction, Nate. I don't fraternize with prostitutes."

"And you think I do?"

Jack had the decency to look embarrassed. "No. I guess not. Although, you did have a reputation in our younger days as a bit of a rake."

"I've changed."

"My apologies," Jack said.

Nate's gaze fell on the woman entering the saloon. "That woman is insufferable."

"Who is she?"

Nate lied, "My wife."

Adeline smoothed her skirts and made her way outside. The

late afternoon sun was warm, but it would soon slip behind the hills. She rode the short distance to the St. James Hotel. After hitching the horse out front, she shuffled inside, and turned into the saloon. The smoke filled bar was darker than it had been outdoors.

Adeline stood still for a second, giving her eyes time to adjust. A hand with an iron grip grabbed her upper arm and steely blue eyes bore into hers.

Between gritted teeth, Nathaniel muttered, "I told you to stay at the ranch."

She put her lips close to his ear and whispered, "And I remembered you are neither my husband nor my father." She pulled her arm out of his grip. "I have no reason to obey you."

He narrowed his eyes and put his arm around her waist. "You're my wife while you remain in this establishment. Unless you want one of these men to make you their mistress. Women don't go wandering into saloons alone unless they are working as a courtesan." He propelled her toward a table.

"Sheriff Jack Garrison, I'd like you to meet my wife, Ada. I'm afraid she had an unexpected emergency which simply couldn't wait for my return."

"Ada, it is a pleasure to meet you." He grinned. "I hope the 'unexpected emergency' isn't too serious."

"It isn't," Ada said.

"My deepest condolences on your recent nuptials to this rogue. I hope you're able to tame his wild ways," Sheriff Garrison replied.

The look in Nathaniel's eyes held a clear warning for her to hold her tongue. "Thank you, sheriff. I'm sure he's had enough of wild times and is ready to be a homebody now."

The sheriff guffawed. "That is my cue to get out of here. It was a pleasure meeting you. I hope your return trip is a safe one."

Adeline curtsied and sat in the chair the sheriff had vacated.

"You will not make yourself comfortable in this establishment. Let's go." Nathaniel reached for her hand.

"There is no need for you to manhandle me." She met his iron gaze.

"Apparently, there is." He took her hand and led her toward the door. "You don't obey otherwise."

"And why should I obey you?"

"You didn't hear? You're my wife. Now keep your lips sealed for one precious moment and let's get out of here."

Nate put his arm around her waist and steered her out of the saloon and to the hotel desk. "My wife and I need a room for the night."

Her eyebrows shot up and panic bubbled to the surface, but she refrained from interrupting him.

Once he finished procuring a room, he led her to it.

"I have no intention of sharing a room with you."

"It's not exactly my first choice either, but what would you have me to do?"

"Leave me alone."

"And let you get claimed by one of those men downstairs?"

Her chin jutted out and she stared at the floor. "I can take care of myself."

"Still defiant? You walked into a saloon after sundown. What possible good did you expect could come of that stunt?"

"I was hoping to find out when the Wells-Fargo stagecoach was coming through."

"Why? Are you planning to leave town on it?"

"No."

"Then why did you need to know when the stagecoach is coming, Adeline?" He sighed heavily.

"Owen and the rest of the gang plans to rob it."

"This information would've been useful for me to have known sooner," he barked.

Adeline lowered her eyes and stared at the floor. Nate walked to the door. He turned back and gave her a lingering look, before walking out, leaving her standing alone at the foot of the bed.

Chapter 4

Nate walked along the river. His eyes had adjusted to the dim moonlight. His fathers words echoed in his mind. 'If your intentions toward her are not honorable then you should ride out again.' He'd heeded his father's warnings and had ridden off again. How could he have known Adeline would follow him? Pa was correct. There was no way he could be around Adeline and keep his hands off her. There was nothing honorable in that, but he couldn't get her out of his head. When he allowed himself to be in the same room with her, she made his blood run hotter and his brain turn to mush.

He sat at the base of a tree on the bank of the river and tossed in a stone. What possible solutions were there? He could get her out of his life and send her away on the next stage coach, but he knew he wouldn't do that. He could no more let her go back to Kansas City than he could watch her hang. His options were limited. She was here. In Cimarron. In his hotel room. It was unseemly. The only viable option was to marry her. He couldn't marry a detective. Could he? Would she want to keep working for the Pinkerton Agency once Owen Glenn was captured? Maybe she would consider raising a family. He put his head in his hands. Once he started praying the words flowed freely and he found himself begging the Lord for direction.

A sound downriver caught his attention and he slipped silently through the night to investigate.

He watched from behind a massive rock as a man dug a hole. The man was mumbling to himself, but Nate watched for several minutes longer to make sure he was alone before he approached, Colt in hand. "Glad to see you weren't blown to bits, Bradshaw."

"You again?" Bradshaw shoveled another scoop of dirt from the hole.

"What are you digging the hole for?" Nate asked.

"Milton didn't say, but I'm positive it's my grave. A favor to Owen. Owen wants revenge for Ricketts death. He blames me."

"Who is Milton?"

"Milton Yarberry. I don't know much about him. Owen

hooked up with him while hiding in the hills."

Nate waved the gun indicating he should move. "Let's go. I think we can help each other."

"He'll think I went willingly and he'll kill me."

"He plans to kill you anyway, so why not assist me in arresting him before he gets the chance."

"What makes you think you'll be able to capture him?"

Nate smirked. "I'm the best at what I do."

"You are a quick shot."

"Thanks for noticing. Let's move away from your grave. It's creepy."

"It is." Bradshaw set down the shovel.

Nate tied Bradshaw to a chair in the sheriff's office. "It's not that I don't trust you, but you did escape once."

"It wasn't my doing. I'd prefer to rot in a cell rather than spend a minute longer with Milt."

"I'll be back in a few hours. I have to go make arrangements with Adeline."

"You caught up to her?"

"Minutes after I dropped you with Jack."

"I thought she'd have been gone by then."

"She wants to clear her name."

"Do you think I can help?"

"Possibly. I'm formulating a plan."

Nate had a few ideas for how to keep Adeline safe, but he had no intention of sharing the particulars with the bandit.

Adeline sat on the edge of the bed. What would happen when Nathaniel returned? It had been careless of her to put herself in this situation. Nathaniel was correct to admonish her. If she hadn't done such an addle-brained thing as to walk into a saloon unaccompanied, she wouldn't be in this predicament. Her heart leapt when he'd introduced her as his wife. She'd noticed how he'd shortened her name, so the sheriff would be less likely to make the connection. He'd been kind to her and did everything he could to protect her and her reputation, even when her behavior had been atrocious. Would he ever consider courting a woman like her? She'd heard the sheriff's words about Nate's character. She wondered if he'd ever been in love, and if it was possible for him to fall in love with her.

Where had he gone? Her thoughts circled round and round

pondering Nathaniel's whereabouts. Did he have another room? Maybe he was in a room with one of the courtesans. He may have returned to the ranch, but she didn't think he'd leave her behind, although it would serve her right for leaving the ranch in the first place. The night grew late and she needed to rest, but she was afraid the minute she undressed and crawled under the quilted coverlet, he would return. Would he expect something from her she wasn't prepared to give? Would she be able to deny him? She extinguished the lamp and rested atop the bed fully clothed.

Her eyes flew open at the sound of the door opening.

"Adeline, it's Nate. Are you dressed?"

"Yes."

He lit the kerosene lamp and stood over her. Her heart felt like it was doing somersaults as she stared at him. "Us being alone together in a room after dark is scandalous, Nathaniel."

"I like the way you say my name." He took another step toward the bed.

"Are you forgetting we're not actually married?" She propped herself up on the headboard.

"I'm fully aware of what we are and are not."

She cleared her throat.

He reached over and put his hand behind her neck and

rubbed his thumb along the length of her neck. "What are we doing here, love?" He stroked her cheekbone with his knuckles.

"You're the one who came into the room. Why don't you tell me?" A nervous giggle escaped. "Why do you call me love?"

"It suits you."

"Why?"

"Several reasons."

"Do you care to enlighten me?"

"Not now."

"Where will you sleep?"

"Where do you think?"

She felt warmth flood her cheeks.

"You look alluring with a healthy blush, love."

She lowered her eyes and stared at her hands.

He took her hands in his and lifted them to his lips. "If you were my wife, I wouldn't walk away. I would do every single one of the things I've been dreaming of doing to you since the moment you smashed me over the head at the river."

Breathlessly, she asked, "And what things are those?"

"To repeat those thoughts to a woman not my own would

indeed be scandalous, my love. Get some sleep. I'll be back before sunrise with supplies, so you can freshen up for your wedding day. Then I will take my time showing you."

He firmly shut the door behind him, leaving her gaping open-mouthed.

Nate leaned against the outside of the hotel room door and wondered if he was making a mistake. He'd heard talk of a circuit riding preacher due to arrive on the stage-coach today. Would she be willing to marry him? If she wanted his continued protection, she'd have no choice. There was no way he would disappoint his father by dishonoring her. Yet, it was impossible to expect him to keep his hands off her any longer. Either she would get on that stage-coach and head back to Kansas City or she would marry him. It was a simple choice for her to make.

He sunk to the floor with his back to the door. His gut twisted at the thought she might choose to return home rather than remain with him. John Bradshaw agreed to give a full account of the heinous things they'd done to her while she was held captive. People would know she was innocent. She would be safe from everyone, but him. She should go home. There was a suitor waiting for her. The gentleman who'd paid the detectives to find her. Was she in love with James Cleveland? She would probably choose to go.

This impulsiveness was not his usual style. He raked his fingers through his hair. His feet nearly gave out under him when he stood. He'd never been given to nervousness. He knocked softly on the door.

She opened it. "What did you mean, Nathaniel?"

He held out the package. "I brought you a new dress."

"What did you mean about my wedding day? Who do you intend for me to marry?"

"Me."

"Why?"

"It's necessary."

"That's not a reason to marry," she said.

Nate walked past her and stared out the window. "Did you sleep well?"

"What do you think? I didn't get another moments rest after what you said when you left here."

"I won't force you, Adeline."

"You won't?"

"If you want to go home, the stage-coach will be here shortly. I'll put you on it."

"You will?"

"Yes."

"What happens if I don't get on the coach?"

"If you choose to stay, we will be married. The circuit preacher is arriving on today's stage-coach. The wedding will take place when he arrives."

"Why would you marry me?"

"I told you, it's necessary."

"Necessary. What does that even mean?"

"I'm not sure I can answer that."

"I wish you would've answered differently. I don't want to get on that coach, but I will."

He drew her into his arms and held her close. There was a heavy ache in his heart. He would have to let her go.

Adeline leaned into his embrace. If he'd said he cared for her she'd have agreed to marry him. Her feelings for him grew stronger every minute she spent in his presence. Leaving him behind would be torturous, but she would not enter a marriage of convenience any more now than she would have before her abduction. If she was to marry him, he had to want to be with her. Not for her protection, but because he cared for her. His motives seemed noble, but she needed him to be fond of her. Maybe even grow to love her.

She'd fallen in love with him, but what did it matter if his feelings were merely protective ones. A lawman doing his job. How she wished it were different. She lifted her head and gazed into his eyes. The passion there was unmistakable. He wanted her, but he hadn't even kissed her. He'd had numerous opportunities, but he hadn't crossed that line. A gentleman through and through. No, she had to be deluded. If he felt any passion, he would act on it, wouldn't he? If he wouldn't, she would.

She stood on her tiptoes and brushed her lips across his. The contact made her insides melt like butter. Pulling back, she studied his reaction. The look in his eyes was unreadable. He grabbed the back of her head and lowered his mouth to hers. His kiss was hungry and urgent. He pulled her body close, molding it against his. After several minutes of passionate kissing. She broke free from his embrace and stepped away. "I will ask you one last time, Nathaniel. Why would you choose to marry me?"

"I need you."

It was enough for her. "Then, yes. I will marry you."

He reached for her again and brushed her hair from her face. "Get changed, please. We'll be married in a few hours."

She remained silent and he pulled her back to him. His kiss was gentler this time, his body more relaxed. "Tonight, you'll be mine, Adeline."

A thrill shot up her spine at the thought of having this man she'd grown to love as her own. "And you'll be mine."

"I suppose I will be." He kissed her once more. "I'll be back in fifteen minutes." He stepped out and closed the door.

How was she to prepare for a wedding in fifteen minutes? She could barely breathe. Would 'need' be an adequate basis for beginning a marriage?

She'd prayed throughout the night. While she'd hoped Nathaniel's reference to her wedding day meant he wanted to marry her, and his innuendo seemed to suggest it was the case, she hadn't been sure. She'd considered running again, but didn't want to leave him. Her prayers had been scattered and confused. She'd asked for clarity and direction. God had gotten her through so much pain and tragedy in the past months. He'd protected her even when she'd willed herself to die. His love was present even when she turned her face from Him. He'd known the end from the beginning and had kept her alive. Was it for this? So she could be Nathaniel Hayes' wife?

Then she remembered her scars. What would he think when he saw them? He wouldn't want to marry a woman disfigured by scars. Would he? She had to tell him. It wasn't fair to wait until they were wed. What if he discarded her? Tears fell unbidden. She hadn't shed tears since the night they'd taken her from her home. God had given her the strength to avoid giving Ellis the satisfaction of seeing her cry. Yet, now the fear of rejection overwhelmed her and she couldn't stop the flow of tears.

She sobbed. Her whole body shook with emotion and she let herself feel the pain.

Nate busted into the room without knocking. "I heard you crying. What's wrong? We don't have to get married if you don't want to."

"I want to."

"Then what is it?"

"I can't talk about it."

"Adeline, if I'm to be your husband, you're going to have to tell me what has you so upset. Did I do something?"

"Yes. No."

"Which is it?"

"I don't know."

"You are raving like a lunatic."

"I know."

"You do?"

"Yes."

"I'm going to hold you now. Is that agreeable?"

"Yes, please."

He pulled her into his arms and stroked his hand up and down her back. "Woman, even in an emotional state, you make me crazy with desire."

"I thought you were 'inured to my charms'?"

"If only I'd been speaking the truth."

"You're a liar, Nathaniel."

"I've confessed my sins to the Lord, and asked Him to direct my steps. I'm fairly certain this marriage is His plan." Nate kissed the top of her head.

"I hope so."

"Me too," Nate said.

"I must tell you something."

"I realize the things that must've been done to you while you were in captivity. I'm not naive. I understand if you're not pure.

I still want to marry you."

"I remain a virgin."

"All those months?" His voice broke on the words. "They left you be?"

"No. I'm a virgin, but I'm far from pure and undefiled. In the early days, Ellis touched me as often as he could. I was tied up, so fighting back wasn't a viable option, although I tried. The more I fought the happier he was, so eventually I stopped fighting. He attempted to rape me several times, but was too inebriated to succeed. I think after the third time he gave up. The others considered me Ellis' property and left me alone."

"I'm sorry you suffered through that, love." He stroked her hair.

She swallowed the lump in her throat. If only he meant it when he called her 'love' so casually.

He continued, "You deserve a better life than I can give you, but I will try to be the husband you need."

There it was again. Need. She did need him if she was being honest, but she wanted a marriage built on more than mutual need. She wanted to be loved.

She pulled away from him, walked over to the bed, and sat on the edge. "I must finish telling you before I lose my courage."

"I'm listening."

"It might be better to show you." She reached for her hemline with the intention of lifting her skirts.

"Adeline, you don't have to do this."

"You need to see the scars. If you don't see them now you'll be shocked later and I don't want to trap you."

"You are not trapping me. I don't care about scars. Except that they make me want to kill the man who caused you pain."

"You did kill him." She wondered if he would still make light of the scars once he saw how disfigured she was.

He didn't mention he'd seen her scars the morning he'd left for Santa Fe. It didn't matter now, they would be married tonight and his improper conduct where she was concerned would be a thing of the past. She would be his. Scars and all.

Time had gotten away from them while she'd wept in his arms. There was no time for her to get ready and join him at the stage-coach. He hurried to meet the coach. When the man carrying a worn Bible stepped off, he nearly exploded with anticipation. Maybe he wanted this more than he was admitting to himself. A man getting married to protect a woman should not be this elated. He knew he was fooling himself. He wasn't protecting her. He was taking her for his own.

He spotted William Pinkerton and took a deep breath. Her saving grace was here. She didn't need to marry him. Her boss was here to save her. Was it a chance he could take? He should greet Will. He was an old-friend who had worked on several cases with him, but in this moment he would give anything to send Pinkerton back where he came from.

"Nate! I'm pleased to see you."

"Hello, Will."

"I came to find one of my detectives, George Nelson. He seems to have disappeared."

"Never heard of him."

Will pulled out a sketch and showed him. "I've seen him. Ellis Ricketts put a bullet in his head in the river by the Pallisade Sills."

"Well that's disturbing."

"I'm also here to assist one of our female detectives, Miss Adeline McCarty. Have you seen her?"

"I have."

"Is she well?"

"She is."

"Would you be willing to take me to her?"

"Not yet. Give me a few hours, would you?"

"That would be agreeable. It will give me time to settle into my room."

"Meet me at the sheriff's office at three o'clock this after-noon."

Nate turned to the preacher. "Would you kindly come with me, sir?"

The preacher followed Nate into the hotel. "I need you to perform a marriage, will you do that?"

"That depends on several things."

"What things, sir?"

"You can call me Pastor Evans."

"On what things does it depend, Pastor?"

"Are you both believers?"

"We are."

"Is the woman willing to be married?"

Nate laughed, but deep down he wondered. "Yes. She is."

"Is there someone who can witness the wedding?"

"I'll get someone." Nate walked off and grabbed a patron stumbling from the saloon.

"This is your witness?"

"Yes."

"I don't think this man is sober."

"Fine. Give me one minute."

Nate hurried back out of the hotel. "Pinkerton come here a moment, would you?"

"Sure."

"I need you to witness a wedding."

"Whose getting married?"

"I am."

"I don't believe it."

"Well, believe it." Nate grabbed his shoulder and led him to the preacher. "Pastor, I brought William Pinkerton to witness the wedding. He's sober."

"If you have the young lady stashed around here some-where, we can get started."

"I'll get her. Is the hotel lobby adequate?"

"It's perfectly acceptable. The Lord doesn't care about the

location. What matters to the Lord is that you both love Him and each other."

The words stung as Nate thought about his growing feelings for Adeline and her lack of anything, but physical attraction for him. She'd probably only agreed to marry him because her father was gone and she didn't want to be alone, but she would grow fond of him in time. He hurried back to the room and knocked softly on the door. "Are you ready, love?"

"I am." She opened the door and it took all his willpower not to pull her into his arms.

"You are the most beautiful creature I've ever seen." He swallowed hard. "We need to get downstairs. Pastor Evans is waiting."

The preacher read a few words about charity and God's design for marriage between a man and a woman going back to Adam and Eve. Then he asked them to repeat the vows. "Do you, Nathaniel Hayes, take this woman to be your lawfully wedded wife? To love and to cherish?"

"I do," Nate said.

"Do you, Adeline McCarty, take this man to be your lawfully wedded husband? To honor and obey?"

Will raised an eyebrow, but didn't interrupt.

"I do."

"You may kiss your bride."

Nate crushed Adeline in an embrace and kissed her gently.

Turning to Will he spoke, "Yes, this is Adeline Hayes, my wife, your former employee."

"Excuse me?" Adeline asked. "Former employee? Was I fired?"

"You're a married woman now. Don't you plan to stay home and have babies?"

"You are an insufferable close-minded cave-dweller."

He smirked.

He saw the conflicting emotions in her eyes. "We haven't caught Owen Glenn yet."

"You can help me catch him, but will you please quit the agency? I don't want you out risking your life."

"I'll think about it."

"So much for your promise to 'obey.'" His head dipped, so he could kiss her again. The preacher cleared his throat. "I'm going to excuse myself." He lowered his voice so only Nate could hear him. "You and your bride should go home where you can be alone."

"Thank you, Pastor Evans. I appreciate your taking the time to marry us."

"Take care of your wife."

Will chimed in once the preacher left the lobby. "You tricked me into witnessing my detective's wedding."

"No, I asked you to witness my wedding. And that's exactly what you did."

"You didn't tell me you were marrying Adeline McCarty. You had to know I hadn't met her in person."

"I couldn't let you get to her first. She might have decided since you were here to rescue her and take her home to her old life, she didn't need me anymore."

Adeline interrupted, raising her voice to be heard above the din from the nearby saloon. "So, you decided to trick me instead of offering me the opportunity to choose to marry you anyway?"

He met her gaze and pulled her a few paces away from Will. "I didn't want to lose you."

She kissed him again. "You wouldn't have lost me."

"I hate to interrupt this precious moment between newly-weds, but I have news."

"Can it wait, Mr. Pinkerton?" Adeline asked.

"I don't think it should."

She pulled her gaze from Nathaniel's and met William Pinkerton's. "What is it?"

"Your father had hoped you would return home."

"My father is dead."

"No, he isn't. He was shot twice, but wasn't killed. Once in the shoulder and once in the hip. Infection made his recovery difficult. After several months, he was finally well enough to go home, but he was distraught to learn we had recruited you for this mission and demanded we fetch you and bring you back to Kansas City."

"My father is alive?"

"Yes."

Nate could see her pain and confusion when she turned to face him. "I didn't know, Adeline. I would've told you."

"I want to see my father."

"Of course. We'll leave immediately."

"But what about the Wells-Fargo Stage Coach? I still don't know when it's arriving and we need to prevent the holdup."

"We will. The stagecoach they are most likely planning to rob won't arrive for another week. We can deal with it when we get back from Kansas City."

She nodded. "All right."

"I'm sorry, Adeline. I swear to you I didn't know your father was alive. I would've planned for both of our fathers to be at the wedding if I'd have known."

"Your father will be angry. Won't he?" Adeline asked.

"No. He'll be glad we got married. He made it clear he didn't want me to take liberties with you."

"Is that why we married? So, you could take liberties freely?" she whispered.

Nate smiled, but didn't answer her question. "Pa was protective of you and was afraid I'd hurt you. I hope I haven't. I never meant to cause you pain."

"It's better this way. My father would never have agreed to this wedding. Now he has no choice. We're already married. He'll have to make the best of it."

"Are you sure? We could annul the marriage."

"I made promises before Almighty God. I intend to keep

them. Do you?"

"Yes."

"Then prepare to meet my earthly father."

"Good luck." Will slapped him on the back. "You have no idea what you've gotten yourself into."

"Are you still glad you married me?" Adeline simpered primly while batting her eyelashes.

He put his arm around her waist and led her back to the room. When they were finally alone he answered her. "I'm more than glad I married you. I plan to spend the rest of my life proving it to you, and I'm going to start immediately."

Chapter 5

Early the following morning, Adeline watched her husband sleep. He'd been gentle. Taking his time with her, he'd traced each scar. He'd told her again how much it hurt him that she'd suffered, but that she was the most beautiful woman he'd ever laid eyes on. She'd believed he meant every word. How had she been so blessed to be captured by a man who wanted her, despite her flaws? God had given her an amazing gift. She had married for love. Nathaniel might not love her, but even if he never loved her, she'd be happy to spend her days by his side.

Nathaniel's eyes opened and he pulled her close.

They arrived at the ranch shortly before noon. Rosa stood over a wash bucket with a chicken in her arms.

"Is Pa around?" Nathaniel asked.

"Mr. Hayes rode-off to town to look for you."

"He knew I was going to hunt for Owen Glenn," Nathaniel said.

"He didn't go looking for you, Nate. He was searching for Miss Addy."

"I didn't tell him I was leaving." Adeline looked away from the accusation in the other woman's eyes.

"Stay here with Rosa while I ride back into town and find Pa." He pinned her with his stare. "I can trust you to stay put?"

"Of course."

"I'd like to give him the news before he hears it from anyone else."

"What news?" Rosa asked. "Did something happen?"

Adeline beamed. "We got married."

"To each other?"

"Yes, to each other."

"This is wonderful news! We will celebrate. Let me call the ranch manager."

"Rosa, as delightful as that sounds, it will have to wait. We learned Adeline's father survived the attack, so we must go and see him as soon as I find Pa."

"Senora! I'm thrilled for you." Rosa left the chicken in the bucket and hugged Adeline. The chicken squawked.

"Thank you." Adeline patted Rosa's shoulder.

"Get going, Nate." Rosa said.

Nathaniel bent down and kissed Adeline gently before riding off.

"What's wrong with that chicken? She doesn't look well."

"A raccoon nearly took it's wing off last night. Mr. Hayes heard the noise and rescued the hen, but she's hurting. We're going to have to clean the wound well and hope for the best."

"Aw. Poor little thing."

Rosa pulled the hen from the water and wrapped her in a towel. "She's got a nest of eggs about to hatch, so I'm hoping we can get her fixed up."

"What can I do to help?"

Nate found his father in the saloon with the sheriff. Nate tipped his hat. "Sheriff. Pa."

"I'm guessing I didn't make it back in time to give you the news myself, Pa?"

"Did you forget to tell me something about your precious, Ada?" Jack interrupted.

"Pinkerton filled you in?"

"He did. I've yet to mention any of it to your father. I'll leave you to it. I need to head back to the jail. I've got Bradshaw in there again and I don't want them busting up the jail once more."

When Sheriff Garrison made his way out of the saloon, Nate took the seat he'd vacated. "Have you heard the news, Pa?"

"Which news?"

"Adeline and I were married yesterday."

"No. I hadn't heard." A huge grin spread across his father's face. "I'm happy for you, son."

"You're not upset we didn't tell you first?"

"Not at all. I was afraid you'd let her get away."

"I nearly did. I'll give you more details later, but I need to head over to the sheriff's office. We've got business to discuss and I didn't want to hassle him about it over lunch. I thought Adeline and I would spend the night at the ranch before I take her home to see her father."

"I heard Andrew McCarty was alive. Adeline must be elated."

"She is, but she's also nervous to tell him about the wedding."

"I'll bet. That girl was being groomed to marry one of the elite. I hear they even sent her to finishing school. She was expected to marry a president's son or a rich banker. Someone of that ilk. Yet, she married my boy."

"I'm not exactly a pauper either."

"No, you're most certainly not. You married well, son."

"I think she'll be good for me. How did you learn so much about her and her father?"

"Spoke to some friends when I was trying to help you prove Adeline's innocence. Once I realized she was Andrew McCarty's daughter, I knew everything I needed to know."

"Do you know him?"

"We've met a few times, but I doubt he'd remember me. He bought some land from us to run railroad tracks through. It was part of the parcel I gave you."

"Is he a man of decent character?"

"Seems to be. He's a godly man."

"I realize I married impulsively, but I was afraid she'd leave the minute she felt safe enough to go back to Kansas City."

"I don't think she was going anywhere unless you gave her a reason to run off."

"What kind of reason would that be?"

"If you had made her feel unwanted."

"I think I may have done so. Thankfully, she knows now how much I want her."

"She's going to need more than that."

"What do you mean?"

"She'll need to know you love her. Women need assurance. Have you told her, son?"

Nate shook his head.

"Do you love her?"

Nate didn't respond. "I'd better head over to see the sheriff. I'll return shortly."

His father nodded. Nate headed out of the saloon and across to the sheriff's office.

"Jack, can we talk a moment?" Nate ducked inside the building. "Oh, Harry. I didn't know you were in town. What brings you to Cimarron?"

"You do."

"I do?"

"I was hoping we could talk."

"Sure. Talk."

The three men sat around Sheriff Garrison's desk.

Harry put his feet on Jack's desk and leaned back. "I'm looking for a deputy. My work is getting to be too much for one man."

Nate leaned forward. "There are a few competent men I could suggest."

"What about you?" Harry asked.

"I don't know. I'm not sure I could stand the stability."

"You're a married man now. Think about it," Jack interjected.

"I will. I'll give it some thought."

"Now about that wife of yours." Harry sat up straighter.

Nate stood. "What about her?" he snapped.

"Why didn't you tell me you had her in custody? I specifically asked you about her."

"She would've been hung. I was protecting her until I could prove her innocence."

"Why did you lie to Jack and tell him you two had already married?"

"To protect her. She came to the saloon alone."

"She wouldn't have been the first woman or last woman to do so."

"And you know how people talk about such women."

"I do. Well, I don't know about Jack, but I would've taken your word if you'd told me she was innocent. We're friends," Harry said.

"Same here. I wouldn't have doubted you," Jack said. "Besides, I knew who she was the moment she walked into the saloon. Do you think I could sit here and look at her wanted poster all day, every day and not recognize her when I saw her?"

"Why didn't you say something?"

"You were set in your ruse, and I could tell you cared for her," Jack answered.

Nate sank back into the chair. "I should've told you both."

Jack stood. "I shouldn't have had to hear the details from Will Pinkerton."

"You're right. You shouldn't have. I apologize."

"Apology accepted." Jack grinned and shook Nate's hand.

Nate looked at Harry and raised an eyebrow.

"You're forgiven. But don't mislead me again. Especially

once you work for me."

"What makes you so sure I'm coming to work for you?"

"Someone will replace me when I can't do this job any-more. I've prayed about it. I believe you're that man."

"So, if I don't take the job, I'm thwarting God's will?"

"I didn't say that. Get home to your lovely wife. Give serious consideration to the job offer."

"I'll think about it. Adeline's at the ranch, but we're heading back to my place once we return from informing her father. If he doesn't shoot me first."

"Andrew McCarty is too refined to shoot you. He'll hire someone to do it for him."

"That makes me feel much better."

Adeline slowly approached Mr. Hayes as he worked with a colt in the paddock. "Sir, can we talk for a minute?"

He approached the fence. "Come on in." After unlatching the gate, he held it open for her.

She began tentatively. "I was hoping to talk about the wedding."

"What about it?"

"I want to apologize for not insisting you be there. It happened so fast."

He ran his hand along the neck of the horse. "I'm not upset about it, Addy."

"You're not?"

"My son made a quick decision and followed through."

She cocked her head awaiting further explanation.

"Nate didn't want to dishonor you." He led the colt over to where she stood. "You can say 'hi' to him if you'd like."

"How would he have dishonored me?" She took her turn greeting the baby horse and it nuzzled her. "He's so friendly."

"Now I know you're not talking about my Nate."

"I meant the colt." She smiled.

"I know." He grinned and leaned back on the fence rail. "Nate is a man. How long do you think he could've kept his distance? You've been driving him crazy since he first laid eyes on you."

She felt her face turn red.

"And believe me that blush didn't help matters. I saw how he looked at you, and I discussed it with him. Told him if his intentions were anything less than honorable he should keep his distance."

"Oh." She stood and wiped dirt off her hands. "He obeyed his father and rode away."

"And you followed. Considering the circumstances, he knew he wouldn't be able to keep himself away from you, so, he married you."

"There were other options. He offered to send me home."

"I know he did. He mentioned it. Told me he was afraid you'd go and was relieved you didn't."

"I was on the verge of leaving."

"Why didn't you?"

She stared at the ground. "He has my heart, what would I do in Kansas City without it?"

"I'm glad you didn't go. I could see you'd captured his heart, as well."

"I don't know about that."

"Don't you?" He smiled. "Nate's never taken to a woman like he did to you. I think he's been subconsciously hoping to find a wife for years, but he wouldn't have married for anything less than love."

"He didn't want a detective."

"Maybe he needed one. God's plan is always better than our own plans and He knew Nate needed a woman who could challenge him. Someone with substance rather than simply an attractive housekeeper. Possibly a woman with unmatched courage and tenacity."

"Do you think I can be that woman?"

"You are that woman. You stayed in a frightful situation for selfless reasons. You are the best woman Nate could ever dream of marrying."

"My reasons for staying weren't selfless," she said. "I wanted revenge."

"Understandable. I'll let you take that part up with God."

"I have. Nathaniel doesn't want me to work."

"I know. Give it time. He has to get used to having a strong woman around. I have a feeling you'll be a huge part of his new job."

"New job?"

"I'll leave it to him to explain more."

"You can be sure I'll ask him. I'm still sorry you weren't at our wedding."

"I'll be at the celebration." He took her hands in his. "I would've liked to have seen my eldest son get married, but I'm glad he married you. You're a welcome addition to our family."

Adeline felt torn between staring at her husband and staring at the magnificent vistas visible from the train window. The jittery feeling in her stomach wouldn't let her rest.

Nathaniel draped his arm around her shoulder and she snuggled close. "What are you thinking about?"

"How I want to get this visit over and get you home."

"Where will we go when we come back from seeing my father?"

"You're full of questions this morning."

"It occurred to me how little I know about you. Will we stay at the ranch with your father?"

"No. We'll go back to our place."

"Where is your place?"

"*Our* place. It's about half-way between Pa's ranch and Santa Fe. The land is mostly wild. Delightfully unspoiled. I think you'll like it."

"How much land?"

"Enough."

"How much is enough?"

"A little over a thousand acres."

"Why do you need so much land?"

"I don't. Pa gave me the land. He expected me to be a rancher like him."

"Are you nervous about meeting my father?"

Nathaniel grinned, but said nothing.

"What are you looking so pleased about?"

"I would be nervous about meeting your father if we weren't already married, but alas, he can't stop the wedding now, can he?"

"No. He cannot."

"Do you wish he could?"

"No. I am nervous though."

"About seeing your father?"

"My father is the least of my worries. I'm concerned for the future."

"Why? You know I'll take care of you."

"I know, but I'll be in a strange place where I don't know anybody. And on so many acres, I'll be alone. You'll be off at work much of the time."

"I'll make sure you meet people."

"Let's change the subject. Tell me about your childhood."

"There's not much to tell. My father raised me on the ranch after the Lord took my mother home to heaven."

She continued the barrage of questions, but gave up after the fifth perfunctory answer. He obviously didn't want to discuss his past.

When they arrived in Kansas City, Nathaniel seemed to know everyone. He led her to a livery where they got a horse. Then they stopped by to see the sheriff. She wasn't sure why she was surprised he knew people in her hometown. He was a bounty hunter, so it made sense for him to know people in many places.

Her heartbeat quickened and the knots in her stomach grew tighter as they rode the path leading home. Correction. The path leading to her father's house. She would have to stop thinking of it as home. Her home was in the New Mexico Territory now. A sigh escaped.

Nathaniel whispered in her ear. "Is something upsetting you, love?"

"No. I'm fine."

"Then I suppose I shall now meet my father-in-law." He brought the horse to a stop, dismounted, and helped her down.

The door opened and she heard Maria holler "She's here! Your little girl is home." Maria raced out the door and enveloped Adeline in a fierce hug, lifting her and spinning her around.

"I missed you, Maria."

"As I did, you." Maria leaned back to inspect her before turning to Nathaniel. "Who do we have here?"

"Maria, this is my husband, Nathaniel Hayes." Adeline stepped closer to him and laced her fingers through his. "Nathaniel, this is Maria. She's our housekeeper, but she's like a mother to me."

"I understand the sentiment. I feel the same way about Rosa."

Andrew McCarty stood in the open doorway. "What's this I hear about a husband?"

"Daddy!" Adeline threw herself at her father and he wrapped his arms around her, holding her close. He kissed the top of her head. Nate stood back and watched the display of affection.

He'd seen the twinge of pain on the older man's face when Adeline nearly tackled him.

"Is your shoulder wound still tender, sir?" Nate asked in hopes of reminding Adeline, so she wouldn't injure her father further with her affectionate embraces.

She stepped back. "I'm sorry. Did I hurt you, Dad?"

"It's fine."

"Daddy, this is my husband, Nathaniel Hayes." She took a step toward Nate. "Nathaniel, this is my father, Andrew McCarty."

"Why don't we go inside?" Mr. McCarty invited. "Are we prepared for tea, Maria?"

"Of course. Right away, sir."

"Follow me." Mr. McCarty led them to a formal room that didn't look lived in. The fancy furniture was not designed for comfort. "Have a seat."

Nate sat in a chair much too tiny for his substantial frame.

Adeline sat in the chair closest to her father and farthest from Nate. So much for counting on his spouse for support.

"So, Nate. May I call you Nate?"

"By all means."

"Nate. What was the rush with the wedding? Why not plan

a formal affair?"

"Honestly, I didn't want to take the chance she'd come home and marry her former suitor."

Adeline blushed and looked away to hide the color.

Nate continued, "At the time of the wedding we thought Adeline had no family left to attend her wedding. She'd believed you were murdered."

"Well, what's done is done. I had intended for her to marry another, but I don't think she cared much for him." He looked pointedly at Adeline. "Are you satisfied with this marriage to Nate, Addy?"

"I am." Her blush deepened.

Maria entered the room with a tea pot and a tray of scones.

"Then I shall be happy for you." He leaned back on the sofa.

A smile played at Maria's lips as she poured the tea.

"Maria?"

"Yes, sir?"

"We'll need to plan a party to celebrate my daughter's wedding."

Maria's grin widened. "Of course, sir."

Nate stole a glance at Adeline. She looked pleased. Her blush was fading and she seemed happy and relaxed. He wondered how much the stress of sharing the news with her father had been weighing on her.

"We didn't plan to be here for a long visit. There is a planned stage-coach robbery. It's up to me and two local sheriffs to stop it."

"Surely, someone else can handle this while you celebrate your wedding?"

"I'd love to think so, but, no, sir. There are few lawmen in the area. We could return to Kansas City after I take care of this problem. Would one month from now be suitable?"

"Addy could stay here while you take care of business," her father said.

"No Daddy. I should be at my husband's side." She stood.

"I think Adeline staying here is a splendid idea. She should stay here where she'll be kept safe." Nate was pleased to keep her out of harms way. He reached his hand out and shook his father-in-law's hand. He could practically see the wheels turning in her head as she tried to figure out how to undo the arrangement they'd made.

He walked to where she stood and took her hands in his. He could feel the tension in her. "You can spend some time with your father. It's been months since you've seen him."

Mr. McCarty got to his feet slowly. "One month from to-day. We'll have a grand ball to celebrate."

He strolled from the room leaving Nate to cope with his agitated wife.

"Why did you agree to leave me behind?" Adeline fumed. She wanted to punch him she was so mad.

"It's the perfect plan."

"It is not the 'perfect plan.' I told you I wanted to be involved in the take-down of Owen Glenn."

"And I told you I'd prefer you stay home and bake cookies."

"You said no such thing. You agreed to let me help."

"I did, yes. But that was before your father gave me an easy out."

"Tell him I'm coming with you."

"You know I won't. Even if I wanted to, which I don't. It would be wrong to break my word to your father."

"But it's acceptable to break your word to me?"

"Love, don't you want to spend some time here with your pa? You thought he was gone. You've been given more time with him. A real gift."

"Don't guilt me."

"That's not my intention."

"Yes, it is."

"Maybe it is, but revenge is your intent. What does God have to say about revenge?"

"Now you're bringing God into our argument?"

"God belongs in everything we do or say."

Adeline took a deep breath and let it out on a sigh. "Yes. Fine. He belongs in everything." She stomped across the room and stared out the window over the gardens.

Nathaniel persisted. "What does He say about revenge?"

"It belongs to Him," she whispered.

"That's correct. He says 'To me belongeth vengeance, and recompence…' so I'm thinking you should leave this in His hands."

"Is that what you're doing? Leaving it in His hands?"

"I'm doing my job, love. You know that."

What he said about God was true, but the truth of it only fueled her anger more. "Fine. Go! Leave me here while you take care of business, but don't expect me to be happy about it."

"I shouldn't have told you I would let you help us get him. I was wrong to do so."

"No. You were wrong to break your word to me."

"I'm sorry."

"It's fine. Maybe Maria can teach me how to knit."

Her whole body was still shaking with fury when he took her in his arms. She stiffened. "Calm yourself, love."

Pulling away from his embrace, she glared at him.

The train ride back was peaceful without Adeline peppering him with questions. Now that she was his wife, he would have to share his past with her. He wasn't inclined to relive the exploits of his youth. He'd once shared details about his past with a former lover, and had seen first hand how poorly a woman could react to a man's past sins. Emma had been happy to share his bed without any promises, but hadn't been willing to overlook his relationships with the women who had come before her. Emma's jealousy burned hot. Shortly after that night, he'd come to know God's forgiveness and gave up booze and women. He'd asked Emma to marry him, but Emma said no. He hadn't been disappointed. He walked away from the relationship feeling free. Now he would have to answer Adeline's questions and hope she didn't react as badly. He found the whole idea distasteful.

When the train pulled into the station, he stopped at the livery and picked up Sunfire. Then he rode off to Cimarron to intercept the Wells-Fargo stage coach. He hoped it was the one being targeted, Adeline was weak on details. All she had overheard was that it was a Wells-Fargo stage coach expected to be loaded with gold and it would be passing somewhere near Cimarron when they planned to rob it.

When he arrived in town, it was late and Jack wasn't in the office. Instead of getting a room at the hotel or the boarding house, he searched for Jack. He found him at the saloon. "Jack. Glad you're here. Are we ready for the coach?"

"As ready as we will be. Harry's in town and brought extra guns and ammunition. He sent a telegram warning Wells-Fargo of the possible attack. They responded that they'd send two guards with the coach. If things go as planned, between the guards, Harry, you and I, we should be able to take down the remaining gang members with minimal trouble."

"Let's pray that's the case."

Chapter 6

Early the following morning, Nate met Harry and Jack at the predetermined location. They'd whittled the list of likely places for a robbery to take place down to two locations. Both had excellent cover, but one wound through a narrow pass barely wide enough for the coach to get through. This location was their best hope of catching the robbery in time to prevent violence and needless loss of life. They'd sent a couple of armed men to the other possible location with orders not to interfere unless lives were at risk.

Nate recognized the ambush when a man came out of hiding with his hands in the air as the stage-coach entered the narrow pass. He stood there arms in the air yelling, "Come and get me."

Nate quietly moved to Harry's side. "It's an ambush."

"They set us up. They knew Adeline heard their planning.

Figured she'd tell us. As soon as one of us moves in to arrest him, they'll come out guns blazing."

"Probably. What do you want to do?"

"Ask Jack."

"You're the one with a wife to go home to."

"So are you, Nate."

"I'll see what Jack thinks." Nate moved silently through the brush toward Jack's position.

What he found disturbed him. They'd been expecting him to come from the other direction. At least he had that advantage. He moved silently back to Harry's position. "One of them has a knife to Jack's throat. They're waiting for us to approach."

"They didn't see you?"

"If they had, I'd have shot them."

"Mighty confident. I like that about you. Let's go get Jack."

"No. You keep your guns pointed on the man in the road, so he doesn't sneak attack me."

"And what are you going to do?"

"Get Jack. I have a feeling we're going to need his help any moment. They planned this ambush, but they're not going to give up an opportunity to rob a stage-coach carrying a substantial amount of gold."

It didn't take more than a minute for Nate to scope out the area around Jack to determine how many bandits were with him. He found three. The one with the knife and two strategically positioned where they could watch the road and backup their comrade.

He approached the first look-out from behind. Using his elbow, he cut off the man's oxygen. The man kicked. Violently. The sound of the struggle alerted the man with the knife. Nate saw him pull Jack's head back, and move the knife into position. Nate shot him in the head. The second look-out ran toward the pass. Another shot rang out.

Nate ran toward the sound, no longer concerned with stealth. Jack followed closely on his heels. The man who'd been holding his arms in the air was sprawled on the ground, a gun in his left hand. Harry held his weapon trained on the escaped lookout. Jack pointed. Nate saw the movement. There were more men behind Harry.

The stage-coach came to a halt and a man perched atop it turned his gun on his fellow guard. He hopped down and trained his gun on Nate. These weren't the odds they'd expected. Nate, Jack, and the guard shot simultaneously. Nate stumbled. Then fell backward. His last conscious thought was of how glad he was Adeline was back in Kansas City out of harms way.

Nate awakened to the sounds of gunfire and the taste of dirt. Someone had moved him. He was hidden in a copse of trees. When he felt steadier, he reloaded his Colt-45. Leaning against a nearby tree, he waited for a wave of nausea to pass. The sound of gunshots slowed. Had someone run out of ammunition? He stayed low and approached the fighting. That's when he realized Jack was on the ground and Harry was pinned down. He shot the closest bandit and moved in close to check on Jack.

"I'm fine. It's superficial. Help Harry."

A woman exited the stage coach with a lever-action rifle against her shoulder. Nate wondered which side the woman was on. He'd deal with her later. He quietly approached the other side of the coach and took out the corrupt guard with a single gunshot to the head.

Nate heard rustling behind him and turned to see what it was. The lookout he'd rendered unconscious earlier was coming out of the woods. When Nate heard the telltale click of his revolver he fired his own. It didn't look like they were going to have any prisoners to take into custody today.

Jack had managed to get to his feet. He slowly approached the woman with the rifle, but was careful not to make any sudden movements which might cause her to shoot. "Which side of this fight are you on?"

"I'm a Pinkerton detective sent to accompany this coach. I was told they expected trouble."

"The trouble came, as expected."

"And you are?"

"Sheriff Jack Garrison. It's a pleasure to make your acquaintance."

"When you're done flirting with the lady detective, can we get these men cleaned up and get out of here?" Harry asked.

"I think I might need a doctor." The world spun and Nate lost consciousness again.

Adeline paced. She hadn't slept well. Back under her father's roof, she was once again pampered. Tea was brought to her. Her dresses were all washed and wrinkle free. Water for her bath was brought in. There wasn't a thing to do, but read. She'd finished "Little Women" sometime during the night and now picked up "The Scarlet Letter." Maybe she could lose herself in the story. She settled into a rocking chair on the porch and opened the book.

She stood when she caught sight of James on his thorough-bred trotting down the path. Maria appeared at the door and beckoned her inside.

Adeline fetched her father assuming James must have business with him. She stood beside her father as he answered the door. Maria opened the door and walked out on to the porch and Adeline's father followed her.

"It's wonderful to see you, James." Her father held out his hand to greet the younger man.

Maria stood with her arms crossed over her chest.

"And you, Mr. McCarty. I wish I was here on pleasant business, but, I have some hard news for Addy," James said.

"You can share it with me," her father said.

She joined them on the porch. "What is it?" Her stomach tightened into knots.

James looked her up and down. Then he turned to face her father. "A telegram came while I was in town."

"And?" she asked.

"It's not pleasant."

"What is it, James?" her father asked.

"It's from a sheriff in the New Mexico territory. Something

has happened to Mr. Nathaniel Hayes." He handed him a paper.

"It appears Nate was shot, Addy. He's alive. You can stay here while he recovers."

"I will do no such thing!"

"You would defy me?"

"Daddy, I don't wish to defy you, but I will be at my husband's side."

"I'm not well enough to travel, and I'm not sending my only daughter off to the New Mexico Territory by herself."

"I could accompany her, sir," James said.

"No. I don't think Nathaniel would agree to James accompanying me." Adeline took a step back.

"I don't see how he has much choice. Either you will allow James to join you or you will stay here."

Maria spoke. "Sir, would you mind terribly if I joined them? Mr. Hayes would be less bothered if a chaperone was present."

"I need you here," Mr. McCarty said.

"Anna would take care of your needs while I was away."

"Send Anna with them."

"An ideal solution. She'll be delighted to spend the time

with Addy. I'll get her."

Adeline shifted her weight from foot to foot as Maria rushed off to get her niece. It was perfect. She wouldn't be alone with James. "Daddy, I'd like to get my belongings ready, so we can leave at once."

"You cannot leave until the train arrives, Addy."

James pulled his pocket watch out to check it. "There will be a train at two o'clock, sir. If Addy wants to be on it, we can make it if Anna doesn't hold things up."

"I'll be in my room." Adeline hurried to her room and gathered some items. She took her mother's worn leather Bible and stuffed it into her valise along with other necessities. At the knock on her bedroom door, she opened it to find Anna standing there, breathless. Anna was a year younger than Adeline. The two had been close as children.

"Aunt Maria said I was to accompany you on a trip."

"Yes, thank you for coming so quickly. Is that all you're bringing?"

"I don't need much. Aunt Maria helped me pack."

"The train leaves at two o'clock, so we need to hurry. I appreciate you joining me, Anna."

"I'm happy for the change of scenery."

When they rejoined her father and James on the porch, Anna turned away hiding her smile. Adeline briefly wondered why, but was too focused on getting to Nathaniel's side to over think it.

"We're ready," Adeline said.

A blinding light disturbed Nate, it took a few seconds for him to make sense of the light. There was someone in the room with a lantern and they positioned it on a table near his head. He wondered briefly where his revolver was. He wouldn't shoot the man for wielding a light, but he might be comfortable threatening him. "You're awake."

"I am now."

"Do you know where you are?"

Nate eased himself into a sitting position. "No."

"I'm Dr. Murphy. You're at my clinic."

"What am I doing here? And why is your light positioned so close to my head?"'

"I'm wanted to see better to check your pupils."

"Why?"

"You haven't been doing so well, Mr. Hayes. You lost a

great deal of blood. We weren't sure you were going to pull through."

"I remember the gunfight. I got back up after being shot."

"Therein lies the problem. If you'd stayed down and treated the wound, you'd have been able to minimize the blood loss."

"And both of my friends would be dead."

"As it stands, you owe your life to the lady detective who brought you in here with the sheriff. She treated your wound and did a fine job of it."

"It's coming back to me. Another lady detective. This one was holding her Winchester on us."

The doctor chuckled. "I'm glad your memory is intact. I'm going to monitor you for twenty-four hours, but I expect to release you tomorrow."

"I have no intention of laying in bed for a full day."

"I don't recommend leaving before we're sure you're healing."

"Sorry, Doc. I'm not about to stay any longer than necessary."

"I'm not going to hold you here against your will."

Nate laughed, then cringed at the pain it caused.

The doctor handed him a bag of supplies. "You'll need to change your dressings and keep the wound clean to avoid infection."

"You had the bag ready. You must've known I'd leave."

"I've never been able to keep a lawkeeper for monitoring once they're awake. I didn't figure you'd be the exception."

"Then why even try?"

"Ethics."

Nate opened the door to the clinic and stood in the blinding sunlight for a moment as he waited for his eyes to adjust. The smell of meat cooking over a fire made his stomach rumble. He needed to eat something to keep from passing out again. He shuffled into the saloon and ordered. About halfway through his meal, the sheriff showed up.

Jack strolled up to Nate's table. "I see you survived the gunshot."

"Have a seat."

"Should you be out already? It's only been a few hours," Jack said.

"It's merely a flesh wound."

"It's more than a flesh wound. I'm glad you're doing better. I'll send another telegram to Adeline to let her know you're recovering."

"Another telegram?"

"We sent one after we dropped you at the clinic."

"We?"

"Sarah thought Adeline would want to know."

"Sarah?"

"Sarah Jones. The lady detective who patched you up."

"Why am I not surprised to find out this was her idea? I'll send Adeline a telegram letting her know I'm well, so she doesn't do something foolish."

"What foolish thing do you think she'd do?"

"Hop on the first train here. Most likely unaccompanied. And without informing her father or obtaining his consent."

"I don't think she'd do such a thing. She seems to be a level -headed woman."

"A reasonable level-headed woman wouldn't have stayed with the Glenn-Ricketts gang after being given an opportunity to escape. Would she have?"

"She was trying to help get them caught," Jack said.

"Yes, and I respect her decision, but it was far from reasonable or rational. She could've been killed. If she did something else foolish, it wouldn't shock me."

"If she hadn't stayed with them, you wouldn't have captured her at the Palisades Sill. If you hadn't captured her, you'd still be a single man."

Shortly into the train ride, Adeline realized Anna was enamored with James. It was clear the feeling was mutual. She wished there was somewhere she could go to escape Anna's constant chattering. It had at first provided a pleasant distraction to Adeline's own thoughts, but as the train ride wore on, she quickly wearied of it. Maybe she'd spent too much time in captivity. Having been the only female there was no idle chit-chat.

Her thoughts kept returning to Nathaniel having been shot in the side. She knew nothing more of his condition. She wondered how long the recovery would take and if he would fully recover.

She admonished herself for worrying, knowing she should turn her cares over to Jesus, but she kept on fretting.

The train flew past scenery which would've taken her breath away days earlier. Now she barely registered the views.

Watching the flirtation between Anna and James was entertaining, but she wondered if he'd been interested in her servant the

whole time they'd been seeing each other. It didn't make a differ-
ence, but she found it mildly insulting. Her thoughts returned to Nathaniel. She hoped he wouldn't be too distraught over her allowing
James to accompany her on the trip. It wasn't as if she had much
choice in the matter. She told herself he'd understand. He'd have to.

Chapter 7

The door to the saloon swung open. Adeline walked in with a young Hispanic woman in tow. Following closely behind was a man he didn't recognize.

Adeline approached the table with a tentative smile.

He took her hand and pulled her into the chair closest to him. "What are you doing here?"

"That's a fine greeting."

"I didn't need you to travel back here. I'm not hurt."

"You certainly appear to be hurt. You didn't even stand to greet me."

"I could have."

"I don't doubt it, but I'm sure you would've been in excruciating pain. Besides, I'm here now, so there is no sense arguing about it."

"But why are you here?"

"I left the moment we got the sheriff's telegram."

"He didn't ask me if he should send it first. Sent it at that woman's bidding." He indicated a woman sitting at a nearby table with the sheriff.

"Who's the woman?"

"Another lady detective. It's becoming an epidemic. Do you believe it?"

"I do. It's a wonderful thing."

He raised an eyebrow. "She's over there talking with him now."

"She's a lovely girl. Is he interested?"

"I think so."

"I believe the feeling is mutual. Look at the way she's touching his arm while she talks."

James approached the table and put his hand on Adeline's shoulder. "Are you going to introduce me to your husband, Addy?"

She made the introductions.

"James? The same James who paid the Pinkerton Agency to rescue you?"

"Yes. That's me. And I was glad to do it."

"Except they didn't rescue her. Instead they hired her and left her in a perilous situation."

"I certainly didn't know they would do such a foolish thing."

"Didn't you?" The stabbing pain in Nate's side was made worse as he stood. He put his hand out to help Adeline rise. "Let's go, Adeline."

Adeline stood. She pulled her hand from his and gave James an apologetic look, before turning back to face Nate. "What about Anna?"

"Anna, please come with us. Rosa will have a room made ready for you," Nate said. "Do you know how long you'll be staying with us?"

"I'm not certain. I was asked to accompany Addy on the trip, but Mr. McCarty didn't say when I should return home."

"I'll send him a telegram letting him know of your safe arrival and asking when he expects you to return."

Adeline turned back toward James. "Thank you for accompanying us, James. I know it was a great inconvenience."

"I enjoyed the trip. I'll see you soon." He tipped his hat.

Nate approached Jack's table and smacked it with an open

hand. "Jack, I'm taking your horse. You'll have to walk home to-night."

The sheriff glanced up from his companion. "Are you certain you should be riding? Don't forget how much blood you lost. Doc Murphy said it would take time for you to recover."

"I can ride him." Nate shook Jack's hand. "I'll have Pa return your horse. Adeline and I are going home tomorrow. Good evening, Miss Jones."

Nate felt eyes on his back as they left the establishment. He turned around and caught James Cleveland glaring at him.

Nate wasn't the jealous type. It was one of the reasons he hadn't understood Emma's fierce reaction years earlier. He was beginning to understand. The thought of his Adeline spending time on the train with her old beau agitated him. Anna's presence was the only thing which kept his anger in check.

"Do you ride, Anna?"

"I do."

"You can take Sunfire. She's easy to ride." He helped her onto the horse, then turned to Adeline. "We're going to take Jack's horse, Bull."

He helped Adeline mount the stallion and then climbed up behind her. "If we hurry, we can make it to the ranch before full dark."

They rode in relative silence. A raccoon spooked Bull and the horse reared up. Nate was able to calm him, but not before he tore a stitch in his side. When they reached the ranch, Rosa prepared a room for Anna.

Once Anna was settled, Adeline turned on him. "What is wrong with you?"

"Pardon?"

She kept her voice low. "You were a complete cad back there to James Cleveland."

"I said nothing untrue." He paced back and forth in the living room.

"Do you honestly believe he planned for some ill thing to happen to me?"

Nate raised his voice and stopped pacing. "How would I know? I wouldn't put it past him."

"You don't even know him," she whispered.

He glared at her. "But you do. Maybe a little too well."

"You're not being fair. You know he courted me."

Pa appeared in the doorway and gave him a stern look before disappearing back into his room.

Nate softened his tone when he recognized the hurt look in Adeline's eyes. "What I didn't know was that the relationship was so close your father would trust him to take a trip with you."

"I knew you wouldn't like it and I told my father so."

"Yet you still came."

"Because I wanted to be by your side. Are you going to make me regret my decision?" She glowered at him, clearly agitated.

He took a deep breath and walked to her. He put his arms around her and pulled her to him. "I apologize. I didn't mean to hurt you. I just can't stand the thought of another man near you."

She pulled away from his embrace. "Then you shouldn't have left me behind."

"Please, love, I truly am sorry, don't do this."

"Do what?"

"Withhold forgiveness."

"So, you get to have a tirade and hurt people I care about and I'm supposed to pretend it never happened. Can you imagine how uncomfortable Anna must've been?"

"No. I cannot."

"You give me an insincere apology, and I'm expected to move on."

He tried again. "Honestly, Adeline, I don't want him any-where near you, but I am sorry I embarrassed you and that I hurt you. I'm not insincere."

She softened a little. "Fine."

"Will you forgive me?"

"I haven't decided."

"Do you honestly want to spend our first night back togeth-er fighting?"

He saw the fight go out of Adeline as she relented. He once again tried to draw her into his arms. She submitted to his embrace, laying her head on his chest, and wrapping her arms around his waist. The throbbing in his side was relentless, but his need to be near her was greater.

She leaned back. "I felt you flinch. Are you in pain?"

"I'm all right."

"No you're not. You're clearly in pain. Riding the horse here made it worse. You weren't planning to come back to the ranch tonight, were you?"

"I was planning to stay at the St. James."

"I'm sorry. I should've realized you'd been planning to stay in town."

"It's not your fault. If it was only you, we would've stayed there, but I didn't want Anna to stay in a room by herself. The hotel gets wild at times. It's not safe for a woman to be alone."

"James was there."

"He wasn't going to share her room."

"No, but he would've liked to."

"What aren't you telling me?"

"It seems the upper-crust James is in love with a servant girl. His mother would be mortified."

"How does Anna feel about him?"

"She's smitten."

"If I'd known this a few hours ago, we could've avoided that scene back there."

"Oh?"

"My jealousy got the better of me. Had I known his heart was toward another, I would've been more gracious."

"You could tell him you're sorry."

"I don't think so."

"Will you consider apologizing?"

"Shall we take this discussion to the bedroom?"

"You need to rest and recover from your wound."

"I can handle a little pain."

"Behave yourself." She lifted his shirt to look at the wound. "You're bleeding. We're going to need to change the dressing."

"That wasn't what I had in mind."

"Sit. I'll go find the supplies."

"I felt a stitch tear. It's probably going to bleed for a while. No need to mess with it."

"We have to change the dressing." Adeline stood with her hands on her hips.

"Fine, but can you be quick about it. I'm exhausted. I would like to get to bed."

"Yes. I'll hurry."

Mere minutes after she changed the dressing on his wound, Nathaniel fell asleep. She extinguished the light, laid beside him, and pulled the thin covering over them both. In the darkness, she concentrated on his breathing. It was a relief to be at his side. He'd never know what she'd gone through since getting the telegram. She hadn't known about the excessive blood loss or how close the bullet had come to his heart, but now she did, she recognized the miracle and thanked God for sparing him.

He'd upset her with his earlier behavior, but still, her heart filled with love for him. She snuggled closer, careful not to bump his wound.

When she awakened the following morning, he was gone from the bed. It felt empty without him. She rose and walked to the window. The sun had risen and the rooster was crowing. It was no wonder Nate had left the room. She quickly dressed and hurried into the kitchen.

Nates father greeted her. "Good morning, Addy."

"Good morning, sir," Adeline replied.

"What do you call your father, Addy?"

"Dad."

"Call me Dad or Pa, whatever is comfortable. You can't keep calling me sir and Mr. Hayes."

"All right, sir, I mean, Dad."

"You'll get used to it."

"Do you know where Nathaniel has gotten off to?"

"He's out in the stables getting a couple of horses ready."

"Ready for what?"

"My foolish son thinks he's healed enough for the ride home."

"Oh no. I saw his wound last night. He needs to rest."

"I'll let you tell him that. He won't listen to reason."

"This is my fault, isn't it? If I hadn't come, he'd still be recovering at the St. James."

"It's difficult to know his mind, child. Don't blame yourself. Besides, hanging around that wild saloon he'll wind up getting himself shot again."

"Do you think he'll listen to you and stay put a few more days?"

"I tried to convince him to rest, but he's a grown man, if he wants to leave, there isn't much I'm going to do to stop him."

"Did he tell you he ripped some of the stitches out last night?"

"He didn't mention that."

"Nate thought it was only one stitch at first, but it was five. He ripped five of his stitches out. How many more is he going to tear out on the way home?"

Mr. Hayes tilted his chin toward the doorway. "Why don't you ask him?"

Nate stood in the opening watching her.

"I didn't see you come in," Adeline said.

"That is obvious, love." There was laughter in his eyes.

"I'm concerned."

"I know."

"Would you be willing to stay a few more days?"

"For you?"

"Yes."

"We can stay two more days. Then we're going home."

"Thank you."

"You must have power over him. Use it for good," Mr. Hayes said.

Adeline giggled. "I'll do my best, Dad."

Nate shook his head. "She doesn't have power over me."

"Sure she doesn't." The older man left the room, but his laughter filled the house.

The ride home was painful as anticipated. He'd longed to bring his beautiful bride home since they'd said their vows. It was finally time and he was fretting over whether she'd like it. What would he do if she hated it there? Would he be willing to move for her? To Kansas City to be near her father or back to the ranch?

Nate took a deep breath to settle his nerves. The man made these choices, and he was the man. He chuckled to himself. If she was unhappy, he'd want to remedy that even if it meant moving away from the home he'd grown to love.

Anna was staying with them until they returned to her father's for the wedding celebration, and he was glad of it. Having her with them would give Adeline the support she needed while she adjusted to new surroundings. The girl's enthusiasm was delightful. He hoped it would work out between her and James. It was clear the girl was enamored with him.

He brought the horse to a stop and Anna stopped alongside him. The views still captivated him even after several years of living here. "Well, this is it."

"The views are magnificent, Nathaniel."

"They are. The Creator of heaven and earth made this place

extra special."

"Yes, He did."

Nate enjoyed seeing her face as she took in her surroundings, including the log cabin with the porch wrapped around the house, so you could view the surroundings from every angle.

"Can we go inside?"

He dismounted Sunfire and reached for Adeline. "Let's go in."

Anna was on the ground before he could help her dismount. "You two go ahead. I'll get the horses settled. I see the paddock and barn," Anna offered.

"Are you sure? I don't mind taking care of the horses."

"You two are newlyweds going home together the first time. I think I'd prefer to spend my first couple of hours with the horses."

Nate chuckled. "I think I see your point. Let yourself in when you're done out here. I pay the neighbors kid, Jeb, to take care of the livestock when I'm away. I think he's fifteen now. He can show you around if you run into him. Otherwise, I'll show you both around the property tomorrow."

Adeline moved a cobweb out of her way as she entered through the front door. "I see you don't have a housekeeper."

"I do now." He laughed.

She punched him in the arm. "It's sparsely furnished for such a lovely home."

"You can change it to suit your needs."

"Don't you mean our needs?"

"Yes, our needs."

"I'd say it is definitely in need of a womanly touch."

"And you're the ideal woman for the job." He bent over and kissed her.

She touched his shirt where it was soaked with blood. "Nathaniel, did you rip out more stitches?"

"I don't think so."

She ripped at his shirt to see his wound. "If you want to get me out of my clothes, all you had to do was ask."

"It's not time to be funny. You're bleeding."

"Concern is cute on you, love."

"You're insufferable. Where are the bandages?"

"In the kitchen."

She went in search of them and when she returned he'd removed his shirt and was standing there waiting for her.

"You are beautiful," Adeline said.

"Not the words a man longs to hear."

"Handsome?"

"I'll take it. Although, I'm not certain a man can be handsome with a gaping hole in his side."

He longed to take her in his arms, but knew she would protest if he didn't let her change his dressing again.

Adeline admired her husband's physique. She longed to run her fingers along his muscular arms and curl up beside him once again, but this was not the time for fulfilling such desires. It was time to wrap his wound and stop the bleeding. "You're going to need to rest, Nathaniel."

"I still like the way you say my name."

She swatted away his hand when he reached for her. "Not now. You need to rest."

"Some things are more important than rest." He stilled while she wrapped the bandage around his body.

Her fingers itched to touch him, and as if he read her mind, he took her hand and placed it over his heart. She could hardly breathe. He gathered her into his arms and carried her to their bedroom. "We can finish the tour later," he whispered. She wanted to admonish him for lifting her when he was supposed to be taking it easy, but didn't want to ruin the moment.

Anna rejoined them as Adeline was preparing dinner. There wasn't much to work with, but Nathaniel promised to go into town soon and get whatever she needed to stock the pantry.

She wandered out on the porch and walked over to the rail, watching the sun begin it's descent. She could see herself being happy here with Nathaniel. Hopefully, they'd be raising a family of their own here. She rested her hand on her belly. Her hopes were high and her spirit soared.

Nathaniel came up behind her and pulled her in close. "You smell appetizing."

"Do I?"

"Yes."

"I guess that's what happens when I spend the afternoon cooking."

"I like it." He kissed her neck.

She turned into his embrace. "This feels perfect."

"Yes, it does."

He released her and leaned over the porch rail to admire the sunset.

"Do you think your brother will come to our wedding celebration?"

"Once we have a date set, I'll send a telegram, but he
doesn't always get them immediately."

"I hope to meet him soon."

"You will. Even if he doesn't make the celebration, he'll
come to see us soon."

"How can you be sure?"

"He's my brother."

"What's it like to have a sibling?"

"It's pleasant now. Growing up it was harder. He was always messing with my stuff."

She laughed.

"What's this your father tells me about a new job?"

"It was supposed to be a surprise. He told you?"

"He mentioned a job, but wouldn't give me the details."

"It's only preliminary. Harry offered me a deputy sheriff
position. He plans to retire in a few years and thinks I should be
Santa Fe's next sheriff."

"That's wonderful news! You won't be running off chasing bad guys anymore."

"I'm sure there will still be bad guys to chase, but I won't be traveling as much."

"Is it safer?"

"Somewhat."

Chapter 8

Adeline was impressed with Nathaniel's skill. She hadn't expected him to be well-acquainted with ballroom dance, but he'd surprised her. Her father interrupted after the third dance, after spinning her around the room once, he reminded her she should mingle with the guests. As she and Nathaniel drifted from person to person, she pondered how she despised social niceties. People could be so fake. Living in the New Mexico Territory would be a pleasant change. No pretending to be someone she was not.

A smile crossed her lips when she spotted James tucked in a corner whispering to Anna, who had a serving tray in hand. Her father should've given her the night off. She hoped his parents would be as understanding about his choice as her father had been about Nathaniel.

The celebration had been postponed two-months at her father's insistence Nathaniel be fully recovered and at his best before they traveled.

She barely knew the people who filled the ballroom. She'd seen some of them at functions she'd been forced to attend over the years. The cavernous space was beginning to close in on her like a closet as people pushed closer wishing her congratulations. Her vision started to dim, and she swayed.

"You look like you could use some air." Nathaniel tucked her arm in his and led her away from the smothering crowd of people. "It's a beautiful night. Did you see the moon? It looks like it's been dipped in orange paint.

"It's magnificent." When they reached the gardens, Adeline sat on the wrought iron bench. "Thank you. I needed to get out of there." She breathed in the fragrant air.

"We will have to go back in before too long." He stood behind her and rubbed her neck and shoulders.

A sigh escaped. "I know."

He came around the bench and squatted in front of her taking her hands in his. "You've been pale for days. Are you ill, Adeline?"

Her eyes found his and she watched him closely. "I'll need

the doctor to confirm, but I believe I am with child."

He stood and pulled her into his arms. "I'm overjoyed, Adeline. I love you."

"I've longed to hear you say those words since before we were wed. I love you too."

"How could you not recognize how much I love you? I wouldn't have married a woman who was no more than a passing fancy."

She stared at the ground. "You needed me. You told me as much, but you never mentioned love."

"I call you 'love' regularly."

"It's not the same," she said.

"I should've spoken the words. Forgive me?"

Adeline nodded, and buried her face in his chest. A moment later, she lifted her head for his kiss. He obliged, and her knees gave out. He kept her from falling. She couldn't remember a moment when she'd felt more content.

"Do you know how soon the baby will come?"

"I haven't had my womanly time since before our wedding night, so I think I'm three months pregnant."

"Why didn't you tell me?"

"You were recovering from a gunshot wound. And I wanted to be fairly certain before I mentioned it."

"And now you're 'fairly certain'"?

"My body is changing. I can't think of what else might cause such changes. I wish my mother was around to ask."

"What about Maria?"

"She doesn't have biological children. I'm not sure she'd know."

"Talk to Rosa. She would love to be there for you."

Her father appeared on the back patio and called out to them. "You two are missing your own wedding-reception."

Nathaniel took her hand and led her back inside. She spotted a man who looked remarkably like her husband and hurried to greet him. "You must be Isaiah."

He nodded, grinning. "Do we look that much alike?"

It was her turn to nod. "You do."

Isaiah shook his brother's hand, but Nathaniel pulled him into a hug. "I'm glad you're here."

Adeline stood back and watched Nathaniel interact with his brother.

Leaving them to catch-up, she joined her father on the other side of the room.

"Are you happy?" he asked

"I am."

"I asked Isaiah Hayes' boss to send him."

"That was kind of you, Daddy."

"That's what family is for."

"Does this mean you think of Nathaniel as family now?"

"He is a fine addition to our clan. You chose well, Addy."

"I love you, Daddy."

Nathaniel joined them a few minutes later and led her back to the dance floor. "You are the most beautiful woman in the room."

"You're telling lies again."

"It's the absolute truth. Thank you for being my wife."

She smiled. "I love you."

He captured her lips with his. "I love you too, my love."

DEAR READER,

I hope you enjoyed reading my historical romance novella, *Lawfully Taken.* Please check out some of my other titles, including my debut novel, *Stella*, the first book in my Endless Mountain series. The second book in that series, *Claudia*, released on December 15, 2017. The third and final book in the Endless Mountain series of stand-alone novels is *Sofie*, which will release later this year.

If you enjoyed *Lawfully Taken*, the most helpful thing you can do is leave an honest review. So, please consider submitting a review on Amazon and/or GoodReads. It doesn't cost anything other than a moment of your time and can be tremendously beneficial to me. Your quick review helps to get my book into the hands of other readers who may enjoy it.

https://www.amazon.com//dp/B079Y861CK

https://www.goodreads.com/book/show/38751760-lawfully-held

For a list of my current books and upcoming releases check out the novel page on my website: https://www.elleekay.com/novels/

Thank you.

Elle E. Kay

https://www.elleekay.com

https://www.lawkeeperseries.com

About Elle E. Kay

Elle E. Kay lives in the Back Mountain area of Pennsylvania. She loves life in the country on her little farmette. Elle is a born-again Christian with a deep faith and love for the Lord Jesus Christ. She desires to live for Him and to put Him first in everything she does.

She writes children's books under the name Ellie Mae Kay.

You can connect with Elle on her website and blog at https://www.elleekay.com/ or on social media:

Facebook: https://www.facebook.com/ElleEKay7

Twitter: https://twitter.com/ElleEKay7

Pinterest: https://www.pinterest.com/elleekay7/

Google+: https://plus.google.com/u/0/+ElleEKay

Amazon Author Central: http://www.amazon.com/author/ellekay

Instagram: https://www.instagram.com/elleekay7/

Goodreads: https://www.goodreads.com/author/show/15016833.Elle_E_Kay

To join the Lawkeeper Series mailing list, please sign-up at https://lawkeeperseries.com/newsletter

To view the other books in the Lawkeepers series, please visit our Amazon page at: https://www.amazon.com/The-Lawkeepers/e/B079MNY47R/

Acknowledgements

I would like to give special thanks to my husband, Joe Kelleher, who encourages me and takes the time to read my work and make suggestions. Thanks also go out to my fellow Lawkeeper authors who invited me to join the series. I'm happy to be a part of the group.

This story is a product of my imagination and a work of fiction. Names, characters, businesses, places, events, locales, and incidents are either the products of my imagination or in the case of actual towns, historical persons, and companies mentioned, they have been used in a fictitious manner. Any resemblance to actual persons, living or dead, or actual events is purely coincidental.

Any errors or deficiencies are my own.

Coming Soon

the next book in the Lawkeepers Series

LAWFULLY CHALLENGED

A K-9 Lawkeeper Romance

by Ginny Sterling

Pulling up to the kennel, Cindy saw that there were a few others already there to get their dogs as well. She wasn't sure how many were scheduled to arrive, only that she was instructed to be there at nine promptly as per Officer Wesson's curt email. She'd been the only person from her precinct selected to be assigned to K-9 duties. A few minutes early was enough time to chug down the remainder of her coffee and dispose of the cup. Getting out of her car, she ran over to the trash bin and prepared to fling it inside, fully intent on joining the others without a moment to spare.

"NAME?"

Cyndi jumped at the loud male voice that barked at her from nearby. Glancing over toward the tall man that yelled at her she did a double take. He was gorgeous. Tanned, dark hair with a thick five o'clock shadow. Rippled biceps that went on for days. He looked like he could have stepped off the pages of a Men's Health magazine. The coldest set of black eyes she'd ever seen stared at her like she was vermin.

"Excuse me?"

"Did I stutter? What is your name, princess?" he snapped as he studied the clipboard. Perhaps Chief Martin was correct in his assessment of Mad-dog Wesson's personality after all? She was the only woman there, so he had to know what her name was. He was just being difficult.

"Well it's not princess, I can tell you that!"

"No, it's apparently LATE or TARDY. Name?"

"Its eight fifty-"

"LATE. Name?" Wesson cut her off again, tucking the pencil behind his ear as he glared at her. She stood there with her empty coffee cup in hand, stunned at the malice directed her way. What exactly was his problem?

"Officer Cynthia Lance, twelfth precinct."

"I don't care what precinct. I just asked for your name, princess." Wesson said abruptly and turned to walk away. Several of the other officers around her held back smirks as their eyes glittered with laughter. She could feel her face flush with heat as her temper rose dramatically. Either way, she wouldn't let this man dissuade her from her goals or prove to the others that she couldn't do this.

Get your copy of Lawfully Challenged

https://www.amazon.com/Lawfully-Challenged-Inspirational-Christian-Contemporary-ebook/dp/B07C2M1FTQ/

Personal Testimony

I first came to know Jesus as a young teen, but before long I strayed from God and allowed my selfish desires to rule me. I sought after acceptance and love from my peers, not knowing that only God could fill my emptiness. My teen years were full of angst and misery, for me and my family. People I loved were hurt by my selfishness. My heartache was at times overwhelming, but I couldn't find the healing I desperately desired. After several runaway attempts my family was left with little choice, and they put me in a group home/residential facility where I would get the constant supervision I needed.

At that home I met a godly man called 'Big John' who tried once again to draw me back to Jesus. He would point out Matthew 11:28-30 and remind me that all I had to do to find peace was give my cares to Christ. I wanted to live a Christian life, but something kept pulling me away. The cycle continued well into adulthood. I would call out to God, but then I would turn away from Him. (If you read the old-testament you'll see that the nation of Israel had a similar pattern, they would call out to God and He would heal them and bring them back into their land. Then they would stray and He would chastise them. It was a cycle that went on and on).

When I came to realize that God's love was still available to me despite all my failings, I found peace and joy that have remained with me to do this day. It wasn't God who kept walking away. He'd placed his seal on me in childhood and no matter how far I ran from Him, **He remained faithful.** When I finally recognized His unfailing love, I was made free.

2 Timothy 2:13

"If we believe not, yet he abideth faithful: he cannot deny himself."

Ephesians 4:30

"And grieve not the holy Spirit of God, whereby ye are sealed unto the day of redemption."

I let myself be drawn into His loving arms and led by His precious nail-scarred hands. He has kept me securely at His side and taught me important life lessons. Jesus has given me back the freedom I had in Christ on that day when I accepted the precious gift He'd offered. My life in Him is so much fuller than it ever was when I tried to live by the world's standards.

I implore you, if you've known Jesus and strayed, call out to Him.

If you've never know Jesus Christ as your personal Lord and Saviour. Find out what it means to have a relationship with Christ. Not religion, but a personal relationship with a loving God.

God makes it clear in His word that there isn't a person right-

eous enough to get to heaven on their own.

Romans 3:10

"As it is written, There is none righteous, no, not one:"

We are all sinners.

Romans 3:23

For all have sinned, and come short of the glory of God;

Death is the penalty for sin.

Romans 6:23

"For the wages of sin is death; but the gift of God is eternal life through Jesus Christ our Lord."

Christ died on the cross for our sins.

Romans 5:8

"But God commendeth his love toward us, in that, while we were yet sinners, Christ died for us."

If we confess and believe we will be saved.

Romans 10:9

"That if thou shalt confess with thy mouth the Lord Jesus, and shalt believe in thine heart that God hath raised him from the dead, thou shalt be saved."

Once we believe he sets us free.

Romans 8:1

"There is therefore now no condemnation to them which are in Christ Jesus, who walk not after the flesh, but after the Spirit."

I hope you'll take hold of that freedom and start a personal relationship with Christ Jesus.